A FUNNY SOCIAL SATIRE

The Quintessential Fat Girl

HINA SHAMSI

This is a work of fiction. Any resemblance to persons, living or dead, or to actual incidents is purely coincidental.

Printed in the Islamic Republic of Pakistan.

Printed: august 2020

Edition: 1st

ISBN: 9789697868643

Instragram: @hinashamsiwrites

www.Infectiousenergy.blogpost.com

Hina Shamsi holds a Master's degree in Business Administration and has taught at various business schools in Karachi for almost a decade. She has a passion for writing about social issues and runs a blog under *infectiousenergy.blogspot.com*. She lives in Karachi, Pakistan with her husband and children.

Foreword

Writing a social satire is my first experience, ever. The idea of this book came to me when for my birthday; I dyed my hair purple. Everyone asked me if I have lost weight, and that I look nice. Thinking, it took two boxes of purple dye and a hefty bill of the salon to finally get people to notice a change in me; surprisingly, the compliments were not about my hair, but my body.

It made me realize that, as a society, we are fixated on appearance, that too, a certain kind of appearance, anything else is just not acceptable. Hence the journey of words began........

For a first-time-writer, conceiving fictional characters was a challenge, but once I conceived them, it took less than nine months to deliver them. This book is a mixture of many fictional characters with real challenges and a generous helping of humor and sarcasm. It is a journey of laughter and emotions, which I hope my readers will enjoy.

Happy Reading!

Part I

To my soulmate, my partner in eating
brownies and *Halwa*.

He's such a sweetheart

April...... summer is here to stay.

9:30 in the morning. I am sitting on my Oak-wood chair, looking outside the window of my dining-room, mesmerized by the Arabian Sea. The alluring sea is the highlight of this heavily populated metropolis, especially early in the morning. Though not among the cleanest beaches in the world, it is still an actual breath of fresh air for the underprivileged (read ghareeb) people living in this busy city of a third world country. Muddy water and black sticky sand, due to the droppings of camels and horses, and a lot of untreated sewerage water which is callously being dumped in the sea by those who run this city. It's comparatively quiet today; very few are seen jogging or taking a relaxing walk by the waves, maybe because of the scorching sun; another highlight of this city called **Karachi.**

After enjoying the view, I look at Ashoo, who is sitting beside me reading something on his phone; his silver-grey hair falls softly on his large forehead, his set-to-perfection beard, and those cute reading-glasses. *Haye*! So handsome. I have begged him to dye his hair, but *tubah hai*! He will never listen. Now I have also begun to crush over his Clooney look. SIGH! If only I was half as hot as Amal.

Our maid, Sughra, brings one fried egg (the label says *desi* but they are actually *Misri* eggs - *Misri* Chicken doesn't need a Roaster to lay eggs. Allah! What is the world coming to)? The egg is fried in coconut oil and is accompanied by a multigrain (read *bhoosay kay aatay ki*) roti and a glass of *ABCLG* juice. ABCLG is our most healthy apple, beetroot, carrot, lemon, and ginger juice that Ashoo and I have every morning. Earlier, only I use to drink it, but then Ashoo's skin seemed very dull, therefore I asked Sughra to make it for

Bhai, too. We start our day with a healthy organic meal.

Ashoo is my husband, the Alpha-male in my life, the father of my two children, Hamza and Muhammad. We have been married for more than a decade now. I was very young when I got married. My parents were looking for a *Shareef, Khandani, Rishteddar* type *Larka,* and hence Ashoo came with his parents to our house and rest, as they say, was history. His name is Ashar Azeem; I call him 'Ashoo'.

As Ashoo is about to take a sip of his juice, I remind him that he forgot to take Moringa powder. See, Moringa is such a miraculous powder, currently, every health-conscious person has made it a part of their diet. It has many advantages, like controlling blood sugar levels, but its main benefit is 'weight-loss'. I had bought a jar of Moringa powder from NECO's, tried it for a few days, but its taste was so horrible that I couldn't bring myself to devour it. Now that the bottle has been bought, and it can't go to waste, so I got Ashoo hooked to it. He has it every morning with water. Such a noble wife I am, worried about my husband's good health and well-being. He is so lucky to have me in his life; can someone please tell this to my *Amma*, who always says, '*Shareef admi hai jo tumharay saath guzara kar raha hai*'.

But I am also doing *guzara* with his grey hair. Did I ever complain?

Talking of weight loss: in yesterday's speech of Khan *Sahab* - Khan *Sahab* aka Imran Khan, our new PM. Yes, I am among those who voted for "*Naya* Pakistan", you all can thank me now, or thank me later, for voting in *dhoop* and *garmi*, as I am a true patriot. Anyway, I noticed how much weight Khan *Sahab* has lost since he was sworn in as our new PM. His sherwani has become too loose. *Taubah*! So weak he looks *na*. Maybe I should run for the next election. This is probably the only way I will lose weight.

Sughra brings in my jar of *Desi* ghee; I take a spoon of it every day with my breakfast. It's natural and helps boost metabolism, plus the Instagram fitness icon, *Shilpa Shetty* has it every day as a part of her diet and look how thin she is. Perhaps if I eat it too, I will also have a washboard stomach like her. I follow her famous **"Sunday Binge"**, consistently. My entire Sunday is full of cheat-meals.

Tink Tink my phone beeps, and I check it. Meanwhile, Ashoo is up from his seat and is leaving for office. If he would give me a goodbye-kiss before going, like the *English people* do, it would be so romantic. But, no, the maid is standing on our head, and Ashoo is very sophisticated.

Tink Tink, one more notification on my Instagram. *Sushmita Sen* is working out with her 27-year-old boyfriend - my eyes pop out of the socket *'27 jee han jee 27'* - and Sushmita is 3 years older than me. But she is so fit *na*, and the boyfriend; what an eye candy. Okay, I need to finish my breakfast, as shortly it will be time for my water and green tea.

Deep in my thoughts about how my life is, and some people in the world are having 27-year-old friends, my phone rings. It's a WhatsApp call from Aambi *Appa*.

Amber *Appa* or Aambi *Appa,* as we call her, is my elder sister. We are two sisters born to Ahmed Ishaq; Amber the eldest, then me Zoya or Zoie as I am often called, and then there is Anaya or Anu, our **'soeur adoptee'.** Anaya is the daughter of my late father's widowed sister. Anu's father, an *Army Major,* lost his life in the war against terrorism, leaving behind a grieving wife and a daughter. Since then, both of them moved in with us. Sadly, Anu's mom also passed away a few years later due to cardiac arrest. Anaya continued living with us, as a part of our family and even when my father passed away, my mom treated her just like one of her own. She gets the exact amount of affection and equal quota of scolding from *Amma,* like Aambi *Appa* and I get. We all are happily married with children.

Many years ago, Aambi *Appa* went to Canada with her family. She now comes twice a year, gets us cool gifts, tells tales of snow shoveling, extreme winters with storms, and the polar vortex.

'Hello, Aambi *Appa*. How are you?' I pick up the phone and ask in a playful voice.

'*Uff taubah*, Zoie, *bohat sardi hai, poora driveway baraf sey safaid chitta ho raha hai* (Zoie it's too cold, the entire drive way is full of snow).'She replies, sounding a bit edgy.

'*Tu bata, sab kaisa chal raha hai? Bazaar gaie kya?*'She asks impatiently.

'*Nahi Appa, Hamza ki tuition sey time he nahi mila,*' I reply, feeling a bit embarrassed.

'*Aray behan, shaadi mein kam* time *reh gaya hai,*' she reminds, '*tayari shuru karo.*'

Aambi *Appa*'s only son, Jibran, is getting married at the end of this year. We, being the cool *Khalas*, have to get dressed and look pretty; after all, we will be the new-*samdheeana* (in-laws) soon. But before we make any *joras* (dresses), we have to lose a lot of weight to look like *Kareena Kapoor*. Deep into my thoughts, I jolt back to reality with my landline phone ringing, I check the caller ID; it's Anu.

'Okay, Aambi *Appa,* call you later. Anu is calling on the other phone.'

'*Array,* ask Anu to call me, too.'

'I will, Aambi *Appa,* bye.'

I pick up the other phone, a breathless Anu says, 'Hello Zoie.'

'Hey! Anu, *saans kiun phoola hai?* All okay?' I ask, feeling concerned.

'*Haan haan*! I am on the treadmill, Zoie. *Mujh sey baat karo, abhi sirf* 3-minute *howaye hain* and I am so bored. Please talk to me. I have to do at least 45 min.'

'*Uff*! Anu *tu bhe na.*' I reply with a frown on my face.

Anaya, being the youngest, and according to some of our relatives, the prettiest among us, maybe because she has a different set of parents, but for the sake of comparison they would always say that. She has three children; until her 2nd child, she was thin as a stick and so was Aambi *Appa.* I, on the other hand, was always the chubby one in the family. Even in my teenage years, I was very healthy, often referred to as *Moti* Zoie.

'Zoie, *yaar mein tou mar gae exercise kar kar kay*,' says Anu, in a somber voice.

'Anu, *pata hai* I went for exercise in the morning after dropping Hamza, and my instructor Surur said maybe I need to increase my level of effort; seriously, how much more effort *yaar*?' I tell her, sounding a bit irritable.

'Also Anu, I have started eating *Desi* ghee now, apparently, all these Bollywood size-zero actresses eat ghee. Shilpa Shetty does in her YouTube video.' I babble quickly.

'What the crap! *Desi* ghee? Yuck, it stinks. 'Zoie, Simone did Keto, and she lost so much weight. But we cannot eat fruits or carbs in Keto. Everyone is doing it; we should try it before Jibbo *ki shaadi*.'

'*Uff* Anu! No carbs or fruit chaat? What a way to live; I can't.'

'Zoie, shut up! We are doing it *bas* its final and you are doing it with me. We have to look thin for *shaadi*. This exercise alone is so not helping; we have to put *taala* (lock) on our mouths.'

'Okay Anu, let's try it. At least we can do it till the wedding, look smashingly pretty and then go back to normal.'

'Exactly! Now you're talking some sense. *Sham ka kya plan hai?* Mall *chalain?*'

Thank God for Malls in Karachi, they are a savior for many women like us. We dress up, do window-shopping and eat a bite in a clean and safe environment, without getting pushed or harassed, plus it's air-conditioned, the only air-conditioning we don't have to pay for.

'Cool Idea. Let's go.'

'*Theek hai* Zoie, 5:00 *baje* Mall. We will share a *Gapa Gotala* (a form of *dehi puri*) from the food court.

'Okay, I will pick *Amma* too, she loves walking in the Mall, it will be fun, but Anu, what about our Keto diet?'

'We will do it from Monday *na*. Let's just buy all the stuff we need for our diet, and then we'll follow it religiously.'

'Yes, right? We have 8 months left for the wedding. You know, Amir Khan got 6 pack abs for 'Dangal' in 4 months, we *tou* have 8 months, we will get 12 packs in this time. *Bas theek hai,* see you at 5.'

Intellectual Snobbery

I put the phone down and walk towards the kitchen to ask Sughra to finish making food for the kids, they will be home shortly and the moment they see my face, they will say, 'Mom! *Khanay mein kya hai?*' See, that's the thing with having growing-up kids; the kitchen can never be closed.

Caught in choosing between completing my article and taking a bath, I choose to stalk a few people on Instagram. I am a freelance writer; and yes, it's a job. Anu often says to me, with such unique and fresh ideas, I should be in New York. Maybe I am supposed to be in another continent. But Ashoo will never move anywhere. He is a true patriot, out-and-out refuses to even try for immigration for any country. But I often tell him, if we move to Dubai, we will still be patriot *na*. Dubai is like living in Karachi, only cleaner, plus we have cricket matches in Dubai. It's practically our home ground.

Bringing me back from my daydreaming stupor, Sughra informs me that Pervaiz is here to pick me up. Pervaiz is Dina's driver. Dina is my #BFF (Best Friend Forever). She and I are friends from school, but I am not sure which class we became best friends in. We went to school and college together.

I pick my phone; she is the next person on my speed-dial after Ashoo. Before I had put Anu as the second person, but Anu never picks up the phone when needed, so I moved Dina up from 3rd to 2nd.

'Hello, Dina. You sent Pervaiz?' I ask, curiously.

'Yes,' she replies, *'Jaldi sey aaja*, coffee *peetay hain*. I have one hour to kill before Zayna gets off from school.' Zayna is Dina's 5 years old daughter.

I scream at Sughra to iron my black *Khaadi* peplum that I recently got from *Pakistan day* sale; now they have a sale on every special day. By the way, I love this new fashion of loose shirts and peplums. Who knew that maternity clothes will become a part of our daily wear? Plus the fashion industry in Pakistan, especially the ready-to-wear, has grown by leaps and bounds in the past decade. They now have size options for the heaviest of us women. Earlier, the heavier women were at the mercy of '*Master Sahab*' and three-piece suits. Now we can also wear trendy clothes due to the diversity of size and design options. It is a good time to be fashionable.

As I walk towards my room to change for our coffee rendezvous, I see Raziya, my cleaning lady, smiling. Oh! I know this smile. Now that I will be gone, no one will monitor her *pocha* (mopping of the floor). *Amma* always says to keep a check on *pocha*, as these maids leave the corners. Ugh! She will now leave the corners underneath the bed and table. *Uff!* What to do? I will observe her tomorrow. No worries, I need some sane time with Dina.

As I reach our favorite Café, Dina had already ordered our usual pet food; the *citrus salad* with *pine nuts, Panini Sandwich,* and *two cappuccinos,* and if we have space, which we usually do some dessert to follow with another cup of coffee.

The thing with Dina is that I can talk to her about anything, from current affairs, to religion, to social issues and even movies. We read up and talk about nearly any topic. She is my person to go to when I need to satisfy my Intellectual Snobbery. She is my confidant. She is with me through sick and sin.

Speaking of sin; they say, '*Gluttony* or *Lust*: chose your sin wisely.' We for sure have chosen gluttony, hence we hang-out at the Café to gulp down scrumptious food and vent out every now and then.

'Hello, Dina. I so needed to step out of the house. Glad you made this plan.' I say with gratitude in my eyes.

'Uff, *haina*! Me too, *yaar. Aur bata kya chal raha hai?*' She asks me, putting a fork full of salad in her mouth.

Dina and I had so many plans; to travel, to open our own advertising company, we wanted to make documentaries for social causes, and the unending list of things we wanted to do as adults. All these plans, somehow, are now just floating in the cosmic force around us, as we are not sure what we do all day long. Though both of us completed our Masters in Business Studies, we have a passion for books and movies. If only we could, we would end up writing book or movie reviews as a career. Sadly, that didn't work out for either of us; I ended up working as a freelance writer, and Dina as a full-time homemaker.

She is the one who pushed me to make an account on Instagram. I don't like to click my pictures as I don't like my nose and I also look fat in them. But she insisted, saying you can post arty-type pictures on your account. Anu and Dina, both introduced me to the magical world of *Beauty Plus*; what an amazing application that fixes your pictures, nothing short of a miracle, I must say.

As we both start to stuff our mouths with Panini sandwich, I notice a small girl of around 11 years of age, wearing a worn-out cotton *shalwar kameez with* a mismatched floral dupatta, standing in a corner holding a small child in her arms. It feels almost like déjà vu, it's as if the same scene I have witnessed so many times in various eateries and restaurants. The laughing, eating, families and couples, the forlorn maid sitting at a distance just close enough for her to be able to attend to their precious offspring, yet distant enough so she is not equal and not a part of them.

It always amazes me how disparity draws an invisible line in the society, subtly dividing the haves from the have-nots, rich from the poor, and on a lighter note, fat from the thin.

Dina, being the bold one with her emotions, looks irate with what she saw. 'Why do they hire kids to take care of kids? its pure child labor. Call it whatever you want, and please they are not better off being away from home because you give them two meals a day,' says Dina, with a disgusted look on her face.

I agree with her, that's why despite being a diehard fan of Khan *Sahab*, I have my reservations about lifting the ban on the entry of maids in clubs. This will give the high-society ladies another chance to not move their butts and look after their kids. We all know that mostly under-aged girls are hired as full-day maids. These poor maids will just be picking wet swimwear and gym bags. They will never be allowed to use the facility. This will inculcate in them a sense of extreme deprivation. To see kids their own age enjoy every day is a mental misery.

Firstly, strict laws should be made against the hiring of under-aged children as domestic help before lifting any ban. The thread of our society is built on such inequality. I am totally against hiring children for any kind of labor work. They should be in school or at home doing things all children of their age do. I often feel angry and confused about the state of mind of the parents who make their children work at such a young age. I should not judge, because I can never know what goes in their minds, or how poverty can alter the entire thinking pattern of a person.

'Zoie, it's tough for most girls, especially if you are from a humble beginning. Girls, in general, have to face many challenges in their life,' says Dina, sounding concern.

'The other day I was reading in one of the scientific journals about infant mortality rates. The survival rate of baby girls is higher than that of baby boys, and among that the mortality rate of *Black girls* to survive after birth is even higher, considering all circumstances. Girls are fighters from the day they are born. They have to fight to be accepted throughout their life. Zoie, it's really hard being a girl, especially in this part of the world.'

I nod in agreement, thinking what good have I done for people in this world? I am so entangled in my own self that to be able to do any good, despite having all the facilities and time never crossed my mind; felt ashamed. There is so much that needs to be done in our society for the woman-kind, and yet those who have the means and potential are so self-centered.

There is nothing worse than being wasted, I ponder over.

We order another cup of coffee and sip it in silence, thinking where our desire to make a difference as young women disappeared. Did life just happen to us? I wonder sometimes, am I slowly turning into a narcissist? Myself, my hubby, my kids, my work, my house, my body, my appearance, all this mundaneness exhausts me day in and day out.

Feeling drained, I say to Dina, 'I so need dessert.'

'*Cheese-cake or mud pie?*' I ask, 'your call, Zoie.'

'*Mud pie* it is, then.' I reply.

Laundry is the only thing that should be separated by color.

For the sake of our Children

After a much needed intellectual session, consisting of food for both soul and the tummy, Dina drops me home and leaves to pick up her daughter from school. I quickly get in my car to pick Muhammad from school. Thanks to the School Mom's WhatsApp group, I was reminded by some sweet mom about the after-school meeting with the class teacher to discuss the kids' costumes for the annual school concert.

On reaching school, I spot Muhammad and ask him to wait in the school's play area, while I go past the main entrance to see a pool of moms already waiting to be called in by the class teacher. These chic moms amaze me, some of them are always in their gym wear; such dedication and focus towards fitness. None of them eat anything at birthday parties, only a few like me are seen with a plate. They are always so well-dressed and fit with skinny jeans and short tops, designer bags, sunglasses, and not a hair out of place. A few nods, smiles, and hellos are exchanged among the ladies before we all are called inside. Ms. Nasreen explains to us the theme of the concert. We are doing *'Snow White and the seven dwarfs'* this year, she announces. She individually hands over to us a piece of paper that has the name of the character our child is chosen for, along with the things needed for the costume.

My darling, Muhammad, would be the *grumpy* dwarf. Oh! He is very grumpy, at times. He will do justice to the role, I think, giggling in my heart. A few other announcements are made, and the meeting is over. We are instructed to collect our children from the play-area. As I move outside the school building to look for Muhammad, I notice Khadija, sitting in the corner with her daughter. Khadija is another fellow-mom. The most helpful among the group of moms I know. Her daughter, Aieza, is in the same class as Muhammad. We often have play-dates together. Both (mother and daughter) are a gem.

But today, I notice a very upset Aieza talking to her mom. As I pass by them, Khadija waves at me. I walk towards her to say hello and ask her if Aieza was feeling okay.

'*Assalam-o-alikum, Khadija.*' As I lean forward to hug her, I notice a teary-eyed Aieza.

'*Wa-alaikum Assalam, Zoie,*' she replies, sounding sad.

'*All okay, Khadija?* Is Aieza feeling okay? She seems upset today.' I ask with concern. Aieza gets up and runs toward the swings in the play-area.

'Yes, Zoie, she is upset about the concert and her part. This year, again, she is chosen to be "the Witch", just like last year. All the kids in her class are making fun of her, for which she is very disturbed.'

'Khadija, why don't you speak to the class teacher about it?' I suggested.

'Zoie, if I speak to the school, they will not give her any part next year. You know how the system works.' She replies with a bit of frustration.

She leaves me feeling sad and glum; glimpses of my childhood flash in front of my eyes. Sadly, things have not changed since then. Aieza is the most confident and well-spoken girl in the entire class. Every year she performs competently in all the school plays, she is a natural performer. But she is never chosen to play the main lead because she is - how do I say it - a bit ... **dusky,** according to *'DESI* STANDARDS'. The fair complexion green-eyed Minahil, or girls of similar profile, get to play princess but never Aieza. She is chosen to play the witch or any other dark character.

I can't imagine the distress of a parent in such a situation. How do you explain this to a 5-

year-old, that you are not 'pretty' enough by pseudo-beauty standards? How senseless.

Why do young girls have to play such roles in the first place, waiting for a man to rescue them? What kind of values are we giving our children at such a tender age? We are, subliminally, telling our girls that their worth is only skin-deep. As if Media and the outside world aren't enough to belittle them for their looks.

This has been the case always. I remember when I was growing up, only the fairest girls in my class got a part in the school-drama or welcome committee for annual day functions. And if you had a few extra pounds, along with a pigmented skin, then you were an outcast for all extra-curricular activities. How cruel was that. No wonder low self-esteem starts from childhood? This mindset or obsession of certain accepted complexion is so an offshoot from Colonialism of 100 years in the subcontinent. We are brown people, we will always be brown. We, seriously, need to get out of this post-imperial syndrome.

Why do we want to teach our children these orthodox standards of beauty? Robbing our children of their innocence and acceptance and turning them into complex individuals or bullies. Why can't we have a princess who is a scientist or a cardiothoracic surgeon, saving lives, and not waiting for a prince to rescue her? These contemporary fairy tales are totally messed up.

And by the way, why is it a woman's job to tame the beast? ***Why is it always "beauty that kills the beast" and never her intelligence or intellect?***

From a young age, we tell our girls that they need to be rescued, by a prince. WHY? Wouldn't it be nice if we encourage our young girls to find solace in their career or passion?

I sit in the corner of the bench in the play-area, thinking how Aieza will be treated for the next 40 years of her life. When she is a teenager, when she grows to be a successful professional, or when she is about to be married; her skin tone will always be discussed despite her achievements.

As a parent, I often get distressed how does a mother handles such issues when she is blessed with a perfectly healthy child? I, for sure, cannot imagine the fears or struggles of parents who have beautiful children with some *special needs*, how they cope in this world, this competitive world obsessed with looks and perfection.

Thinking about Aieza, I realize how real and harsh *'Body-Shaming'* is? It is the bitter reality we have been ignoring for many years. Do we even realize that Body Shaming is everywhere? Let's just stop for a minute and think about how often we are told to change our appearance? Social media and magazines constantly offer videos and tips about how to lose weight "in days", appear slimmer or fairer "instantly," and hide our "imperfections" without actually knowing anything about us, much less our appearance. Media, so frequently, use overweight as dumb and unattractive, remember the fat geeky friend of the heroine in movies. Every time we enter a salon for services, we are pitched fairness facials by the not-so-fair parlor girl, telling us how our skin will look 10 years younger or brighter. Dermatologists offer fairness shot. Ever wondered how all these celebs became so artificially white suddenly?

We are conditioned to only appreciate a *certain kind of beauty*. We all are beautiful in our own way, but our default setting makes it easy for us to forget that. Our thoughts are molded by our social structures, and the information we are fed from the surroundings. The mind gobbles up unrealistic ideals and projects them onto the body. Our body is what we perceive it to be. **If we hate the way we look, it's because we are told so by our society that we are not good enough to fit in.**

"Workout because you love your body, not because you hate it."

Squat & Hold

May..... let it sweat.

Nothing is worse than going to bed at night, only to wake up still feeling exhausted. Mornings are always lazy for me; maybe I need to pay attention to my habits that zap my energy. I quickly dress up for my exercise routine and after breakfast, I drop my kids off to school and hurry to attend my morning HIIT (high-intensity interval training) session. They say it's good to exercise first thing in the morning as your mind is not awake enough to know what it's doing. I walk in the room full of ladies in their perfect gym wear, holding a water bottle in their hands. An exceptionally thin instructor greets us and she begins an hour-long session to torture our FAT cells. Some of us have more cells than others.

'Okay, ladies! We need to increase our level of effort,' says the trainer with a lot of enthusiasm.

'We will work on those pouches and glutes.' She screams to wake everyone up.

Glutes are the muscles located inside one's buttocks; they are regarded as the strongest muscle in the human body. Many of the pear-shaped ladies, like myself, have to work extra hard on our glutes.

The training begins with the usual warm-up and stretching exercises, a bit of cardio to get the sleepy heart going, and then targeted areas.

'Squat, ladies! Slowly squat down, and now hold!' says Suroor, 'hold it, suck in all those muscles and feel the burn, we are staying in this position for 60 seconds.'

My God! These are probably the longest 60 seconds of my life, accompanied by looking at me squatting in the mirror.

I look at my instructor; she is very sweet and encouraging, until she makes us do "burpees". Seriously, who invented this crazy exercise called burpees? In *Naya* Pakistan, Khan *Sahab* should ban "burpees". I really like Khan *Sahab;* he is so fit.

While I am squatting and holding all my urges; I notice something wrong with the gym mirror; I somehow look so bloated in it. At home, I look pretty toned. Is it a mirror or a magnifying glass, I wonder? Is It a conspiracy by the gym, as to no matter how much we work out, we will always look bloated, I think laughing in my mind?

'FASTER! FASTER, last exercise mountain climbers. Remember, its mind over body,' screams Suroor with a serious face.

My mind is wandering in so many directions, mostly looking at the big clock in the room, calculating how many seconds left. I am making my own conspiracy theories about the gym, no surprise I am not a size-zero yet. If I could have my mind and my body synchronized while exercising, ugh, or maybe if I hypnotize my fat cells into losing their storage. Oh my God! My mind is so not in my control.

After torturing my stubborn fat cells for 60 minutes, I finally sit in a corner to sip my water, absolutely oblivious of my surroundings. The sweat drops dripping from my forehead and my burning butt makes it impossible for me to sit straight. Laughter in the background disturbed my 'Zen state of mind'.

'It's a chia seed pudding,' announces Sasha, a hottie who is a regular in the HITT class. I don't know what her actual name is; everyone calls her Sasha.

Chia seed is from our desi *Tukhmalanga* family of seeds. We had it in our regular stores forever, but it became such a cool thing when its English name was discovered by us a few years back. It is apparently very healthy and good for weight loss, says who? I seriously have no clue, but all the ladies are taking it these days.

Sasha is holding a mason jar in her hand and eating something out of it. She is telling all the girls how she eats coconut & kiwi fruit chia pudding as her post-workout snack for energy. She does intermittent fasting.

INTERMITTENT FASTING—hmmm - I quickly grab my phone to Google about it, so I can add my two cents to this conversation, too. I absolutely love Google; it has answers to all my questions. If Google was a man, I surely would have married him. Intermittent Fasting is when you are fasting certain hours of the day and have a small eating window during the day. Thank God for Google, I think. Sasha says it really helped her get in shape.

Fasting—hmm, I reflect on. But God already commanded us 1400 years ago, when fasting was made compulsory. In fact, there is some form of fasting in every religion in the world.

Maybe I should turn to GOD for my weight loss issues. Is it a sign from the higher-above? I ponder, sipping my water, unable to make any contribution to the surrounding conversation. The soreness of my body has turned me absolutely numb. Under a spell of insurmountable inertia, I continue to sit in silence…..

"A culture fixated on female thinness is not an obsession about female beauty, but an obsession about female obedience. Dieting is the most potent political sedative in women's history; a quietly mad population is a tractable one."

(The beauty Myth, Naomi Wolf)

Fat is the new FAD

While coming back home, I search a few more sites about Intermittent Fasting. I think if I am able to do it for one month, I can do it for an entire year, too. This should be easy.

I am inclined to try it but I had promised Anu that I will do Keto with her. She will kill me if I tell her that I will not be her diet partner.

So I come up with a plan. I will do Keto with Anu and, for myself; I will combine Keto with Intermittent Fasting. The Keto foods will be my meal during the small space of eating, and the rest of the day I will just drink water. That's what you call killing two birds with one stone. I admire my brilliance and smile convincingly.

Sitting in the car, I message Anu from my phone,

'Are you ready to be my diet partner?'

'Let's hit Agha's supermarket in the evening, to pick up the Avocados and Coconut oil, I'm excited to begin this. I can already see myself as a size 8!'

'Let's do it,' Anu replies excitedly, 'I am so glad we are doing this together. You are the only one who can keep me on track and motivate me.'

'I know,' I say grinning, 'I have been a born leader.'

'*Err*, one word of caution, though,' Anu says, hesitatingly, 'Size 8 is too much, don't keep unrealistic expectation, or as they say, you'll feel really low at the end.'

I roll my eyes.

Zalim Duniya

Do you guys also have those uncles and aunts, who in childhood use to call you fat, and 40 years down the road they still do it?

Yes, those relatives whom you dread meeting. I have an uncle who took evil-pleasure in fat-shaming me when I was a kid. He still gets a kick out of it 40 years later. Sadly, Karma works in mysterious ways; the same uncle has a super-thin wife after having half a dozen kids, and now his daughters are also taking after their mother. What kind of twisted Karma is this?

Usually, fat-shaming is never direct; it is wrapped in crude humor, or unasked health advice for example if they see an ice-cream in your hand, they will make it a point to tell you it has sugar in it and how sugar is so bad for you. All conversation with you will be about your weight and never about anything else. They will comment on how much you have lost or gained since they last saw you. There will be comparisons with other people in the family as to how pretty or young that person looks, but it will all boil down to one thing only—yes, you guessed it right -*weight.*

♣

Today, it's our monthly family get-together. All my uncles, aunts, and cousins, along with their respective families, meet once a month. My family comprises serious foodies; they will tell you exactly what part of goat or cow meat will go in which dish. If they could have it their way, they would build a *tandoor* on the table to eat piping hot *Naans.* After consuming heavy loads of desi cuisines, they will squeeze a lemon in their 7up to push it down their colon. But what's amazing is that after violating all possible animal rights through their lavish cuisines and becoming the worst nightmare for PETA, they only talk about weight. They are a fine example of humbugs. Thin members of the family are body shamed for being too thin, and fat for being too fat. If a woman is thin after having a bunch of kids, she is praised and is considered an example for all. This is what we call '*double standards*'.

There are many ladies, including me, who just brush it off when they are body shamed, as a defense mechanism, to show that they don't care.

Then there is that one *thin cousin* who keeps calling herself fat; talks mundanely about her "*healthy eating*". How she gave up carbonated drinks, sugar, or other such blessings of life and doesn't miss them. Before the rest of us can take a single bite of our food, she would scream, '*Uff bohut kha liya bas bohut khaa liya*' (how full she is and how much she ate today). She will then become a self-appointed spokesperson for the rest of us and give long sermons about overeating. A list of *totkas* (remedies) will be exchanged for quick and effective weight loss. And this will happen at every get-together. Sigh!

Since they are family, we have no other option but to love them, because blood is thicker than water. They may be a bit over the top, but meeting with them is often a lot of fun, too. I often thank Allah for this blessing.

Today, the same scenario happens. I sit on the sofa along with my younger cousin; Saba. Saba was also a healthy baby from childhood and was often called *"golu molu"*. Sadly, she is 31 and is still called that.

Saba and I are eating our dinner and having a conversation about the parallel education system in Pakistan. We both walk towards the table where food is kept. I put my plate in the corner and grab a tissue to wipe my hands. Saba leans towards the table to take a second helping of the rice. One of our mutual cousin, Pinky, who's standing by the table, says, 'Saba, why don't you take the whole platter, the plate is too small for you.' a few laughs followed her nasty comment by the people who are standing nearby. But the loudest laugh among those is that of Saba herself.

I have never heard a laugh so full of disgrace and humiliation; a laugh so hollow and sad. I stand there stunned, reckoning how spiteful humor can be. Saba quickly keeps her plate down and with a big ear to ear grin, moves toward the other room.

That day, for the first time, I notice Saba. I had seen her many times but never noticed her. She has the most beautiful, flawless skin and light-hazel eyes. She has done remarkably well in her studies and is such a kind-hearted soul. Today, I appreciate how beautiful and attractive her eyes are. She has a warm smile that can melt your heart, I muse, and 'all this has no value because she has a few extra kilos'. I am all for *healthy eating* and *exercising*. Good health surely increases the quality of your life. I have seen many skinny people who are the unhealthiest. But sometimes, no matter how hard you try, you have a certain body type, skinny or fat, both come under this.

Many have a weak will-power that makes you cheat more than others who have iron will-power and discipline. Should Saba be shamed for having a weak will-power? Should her looks always define her worth? I wonder if Saba had given a befitting reply to Pinky, everyone would have stepped in to say that it was a joke and that she should not take it to her heart. Why does humor always have to be about ridiculing one's physical appearance? Why does anyone believe that making people ashamed of their bodies, by mocking, is a potent way of motivating them to transform themselves?

After reaching home that day, I felt exasperated and kept thinking about the worth of women. How society has made standards for us. According to these standards, all women should look identical, fair, extremely thin, doe-eyed beauties with silky hair, green eyes, pretty much like the *Snap-chat filters* we all use. But does nature also want us to look like that? We, women, spend most of our lives trying to defy age, how we were in our late teens or early 20s, but age will come. And with age and experiencing the process of procreation, we change physique as well. It would be nice if we all recognize it and find acceptability with what nature has given. We can never turn back the clock; it's foolish to think we can.

I want to be pretty not beautiful

I can't find my sunshades. Sughra and I have looked around the entire house, but we are unable to locate them. Today I am in no mood to wear contacts or makeup, and I have to step out to pick Muhammad from school. Powered sunshades are such a blessing; no need to wear contact lenses, they also hide the puffy eyes without makeup. It's no surprise all these stars and celebrities wear their sunglasses at night, too.

A simple lip color along with sunshades, and I am good to go. Poor Sughra; she always helps me find things. Finally, she found them near the microwave in the kitchen. How did they get there? I have no clue. I am about to leave the house when my cell phone rings. The caller ID flashes: "Khadija - Aieza's mom". That's the thing with us moms; our child's name becomes our surname or identity.

'Hello, Khadija!' I say, picking up the phone.

'Hello, Zoie. How are you?'

'Good, Alhamdulillah, how about you?'

'Zoie, I need a huge favor from you.'

'*Haan*, please, *bolo.*'

'I am at the *Aga Khan* Hospital for my appointment with my endocrinologist. You know about my thyroid issues, *na.*' She replies, sounding mellow.

'Oh yes. All okay, Khadija?' I ask with empathy.

'Yes yes, it's just my follow-up checkup. But my turn has not come yet, and I don't want to miss this appointment as the next one will be after one month.'

'*Uff!* We need more doctors in this country.' I say, sounding irritable.

'Zoie, can you please pick Aieza today and take her to your house? As soon as I am done, I will pick her from your place.'

'Oh sure. No problem at all.'

'Thanks a lot, Zoie, I owe you one.'

'Oh, come on! Don't be ridiculous, Khadija. No issues at all.'

'I will call the school to inform them that Aieza will be going home with you today. Thanks again, Zoie.'

I put the phone down and make my way out. I call out for Sughra: '*Sughra*, fry some nuggets and make some noodles as well. Muhammad baba *kay dost aa rahay hain.*'

'Thank you, Aunty, the noodles are very yummy,' says the cute Aieza, sitting across the table from me. After finishing her food, Aieza gets up to keep her plate in the sink. I raise my brow and give Muhammad a look which he completely ignores.

What a well-mannered and nice girl Aieza is, I think on. Khadija has raised her so well.

After much staring Muhammad says, 'okay, I am picking my plate too, mom.' He rolls his eyes to his forehead. *Uff* such a drama queen he is. Takes after his *Phupho,* I think.

After finishing lunch, I make Aieza and Muhammad pray *Zuhar salah* with me in the other room. Khadija had texted me 5 times to say *'Thank you'* and give me an update about the situation in the clinic.

Muhammad goes to the living room to sit with his brother and watch him play FIFA on PS4, hoping he will someday be kind enough to let him hold the controller. "Dream on," I say to Muhammad. Aieza and I go towards my room to have some girl-to-girl time.

'So Aieza, how is school? What else do you like doing?' I ask, trying to be friendly.

'Aunty, I love doing makeup but mommy doesn't allow me. She says you are too young.' She replies as any 5-year-old would.

'You know, mommy is right, Aieza.' I sound like my mother.

'I love painting nails and brushing my mommy's hair, I watch her when she wears lipstick.' She says sounding dreamy.

'Why don't I paint your nails and will remove the color before mommy comes to pick you. We can both comb each other's hair and have our own girls' party.' I offer.

'Can we do that? Supercool.' She replies with wide and shiny eyes.

I paint her nails lilac using my Essie nail color and comb her luscious curly hair.

She smiles at me with admiration

'Aieza, you look beautiful.' I say, smiling at her reflection in the mirror. She turns towards me blankly and says something that made me absolutely speechless.

'No aunty', **"I want to be pretty, not beautiful."**

'What do you mean, Aieza?' I come out of my stunned silence and ask her, 'isn't beautiful also amazing? Your smile, your hair—they're so beautiful!' I smile as I stroke her curly hair. 'You are very beautiful Aieza don't let anyone tell you otherwise,'.

'Aunty, I know I don't look as nice as Minahil and Zara in my class, or like my cousin Soha,' Aieza speaks softly, *they are pretty and so fair with long, straight hair. No wonder Minahil always gets to be the princess in all the school plays.*'

'Everyone tells me I am beautiful; my smile, my eyes,' she trails off, 'But you know what, Aunty? Sometimes, I don't want to be beautiful. I just want to be pretty.' Aieza pours her heart out and breaks mine into a hundred pieces.

I feel so sad for this beautiful, angel-like child in front of me who, at this tender age, is dealing with the misery of body shaming. Aieza's words so aptly convey the feelings buried deep inside the subconscious of many women who want to be *"pretty, not beautiful"*. Beauty is something you have no control over. Like the beauty of the sky or a smile. Whereas prettiness is something you have to work to achieve. Prettiness gives you *supercilious power* over others. It ignites jealousy.

All of us have an innate desire to stand out from the crowd, to be different, and to be the best. I realize why I don't like what I see in the mirror; it's because deep down I was always searching for prettiness, while all my life I was beautiful. Every picture I take needs fixing: from cropping the face and smoothing out my skin to using filters to produce a picture that barely resembles me. What is all this effort for? Who am I trying to please? I often think why are women under the obligation to look pretty 24/7? It really is too much. Sometimes you just need to give being pretty a break. Pretty should not be the rent we women pay for our existence in this world.

What do chameleons and keto addicts have in common? They both eat only protein and their breath is worse than their bite.

(Twinkle Khanna)

The evil Carbs

Late at night, unable to sleep, I Google more about Keto to find out that it requires one to count the number of Macros consumed. Hmm... 'How to calculate Macros' is my next search:

"To calculate macros, first, you need to know how many calories you eat each day. Next, determine your ideal ratio, and then multiply your total daily calories to your percentage. Finally divide calorie amounts by its calorie per gram-number."

I read the above thrice trying to figure out what it actually means. Failing miserably in math at school I wonder if I am still eligible to do keto.

Day 4 of my Keto cum Intermitted Fasting:

At 6:30 in the morning, I scream at the kids for not getting up. When Ashoo asks me to relax, I squawk at him and that ends up in a big fight to the point where we both want to call it quits, till Sughra comes in half an hour late, for which I roar like a wild beast.

I feel so cranky and upset. What is it? It's not that time of the month. What is it, then?

I take in that I am having withdrawal symptoms. I am missing carbs. Oh, God! Being a *carboholic*, I totally miss carbs. But on Facebook, women made keto sound so easy. I wonder if all those comments are real. Who knows, they are writing them while eating croissants or yummy brownies. Also, I can eat a steak but not a banana or an apple is something my mind is not accepting.

My body is so not going in this Ketogenic or whatever state it is supposed to go in. I open the fridge and closed it, trying to resist the temptation of not snacking on something crazy. It's like how some girls only fall for **bad boys**. Well! "Carbs" are like those *bad boys* in my story.

Hmmm - the aroma of fresh *Rotis,* which Sughra is making for the kids, is mind boggling. *Uff!* I just hate myself. Women have done this and gotten amazing results whereas I am glutting over the smell of fresh *Rotis.* I am such a failure, I tell myself.

In my self-abhorrence phase, I decide to confide in Anu. I pick up the phone and call her.

'Hello, Anu.'

Before I could utter a word about my lack of self-control, she says, '*Yaar* Zoie, *bhai mujh sey na hogi yeh.* I miss eating fruit-*chaat* and *pani puri. Bas* 4 *din* and I am so done.'

Suddenly I feel so good inside, knowing that I am not the only one who has failed at it rather miserably.

'*Uff* Zoie, I went crazy, got for myself some Almond flour and coconut oil and God-knows-what; that is fed to the birds. I am pooing like a bird, too. *Please take all this stuff from me.*' She sounds obnoxious.

'Really? Anu, I *tou* am truly enjoying my keto so far. I feel so light.' I lie devilishly smiling.

'Wow, Zoie! I so admire you, you are so strong. *Kaisay kar rahe ho*?' There is envy in her voice.

'Just be strong. See, Anu, it's all in the mind, you got to train your mind first. Send me the Almond flour and all the stuff if you are not using it. But only send if you don't need it.' I ask her without sounding too keen.

'Yes, yes please, I am sending my driver. Take it from me. *Haye*! Zoie, you are so at it. I am so jealous of your will-power. You were always the strong one among us.'

'Well! If you insist, I will only take the stuff because you are giving it yourself.' I say with a straight voice.

After putting down Anu's phone, I ask Sughra to make fresh *Bhoosay ki roti* for me, accompanied by piping hot *daal* and a teaspoon of *desi* ghee—yum. Maybe I should take it slow, I tell myself: *One Keto meal a day - hmm - maybe dinner, so Ashoo can also see how hard I am trying.* I ask Sughra to be alert; Anu *baji*'s driver is bringing *Aata* (almond flour). I Google a few recipes in which Almond flour is used, make a mental note that I will make something exotic for dinner as soon as Anu sends me the stuff.

Sughra asks me if I want to try the Chowmein she made for the kids. I say yes, only in a small bowl. See, portion-control is the key. Eat everything but in moderation, I tell myself. And speaking of moderation, I ask Sughra to give me half a glass of Diet Coke; only half a glass.

Suddenly the door-bell rings. Thinking it is Anu's driver, I open the door. To my surprise, it's Ashoo's *Khala*'s driver. He hands me over a box, beautifully wrapped in dull gold paper with ribbons surrounding it. I open it, paying attention to the detailed wrapping; it's a box of *mithai* (sweets). I take the box, place it on the table and pick my phone to call Dolly *Khala.*

After a quick conversation with Dolly *Khala,* I put the phone down and carefully open the box. Inside the box are yummy *Gulab Jamons* with half a pistachio placed beautifully on top of each piece. Dolly Khala had informed me that her daughter got engaged, and this is the *mithai* that the groom's family had sent.

Such a joyous occasion in the family, I think. I will only eat half a *Gulab Jamon* as you know 'portion-control is the key'.

10 minutes later - I have eaten one and a half.

Realizing what a disaster I am when it comes to self-control, I get absolutely furious.

Uff! Why do they send *mithai* to everyone? It's too much sugar. Spoiling people's diet and playing with their health. Ashoo's side of the family always does this to me. They are the reason for my failed diet. I feel so angry. Now they have messed my 4 *din ki mehnat*- aagh! In-laws, I scream, rolling my eyes to my forehead.

Mirror Mirror on the Wall

August ..... Not a drop of rain YET!

9:00 in the morning, I am reading the news on my phone, it's mid of August and the temperature in Karachi is still unbearable.......

"*Leave me alone*", Celine Dion responds to those shaming her for 'slimmer looks' - the latest victim of body-shaming; reads the headline of an article from a popular Hollywood blog. I click the link to see how the beautiful singer looks; to my surprise, she is unrecognizable now. She was so beautiful with a soul searching voice. Why did she lose all this weight? Oh my God! Why and how I ask myself.

I scroll down to read the entire piece. The blog quotes her: **"I am doing this for me. I want to feel strong, beautiful, feminine, and sexy".** Dion had told *The Sun* and *Dan Wootton* in an interview with podcast.

'Taubah, she looks *beimaar.'* I pass a comment, looking at Ashoo who is busy on his phone and pays no attention to my blabbing. 'Ashoo Look!! My GOD! Look at Celine Dion, she was so beautiful earlier, what has she done to herself.'

He looks up towards my phone and asks, 'Zoie, is it a new picture or old?' I tell him it's a recent picture, *'look how thin she is now.'* He gives a look of disbelief and goes back to scroll his phone.

I take a screenshot of the picture from the article and immediately WhatsApp it to Anu and Aambi *Appa.*

Anu immediately replies, saying, 'OMG! What happened to her?'

'She wanted to look sexy.' I text her back immediately.

'Really? And all these years we thought she was the epitome of sexy, guess she didn't think of herself that way.'

'True.' I reply.

I forward the same picture to Dina. She instantly replies, '*Isko kya howa.*'

I quickly write, 'She lost all that weight to look sexy.'

'Seriously! *Itna wazan kaun kam karta hai?* (Who loses so much of weight?) *Pagal!* She doesn't look nice at all.'

Never thought losing weight would make you look bad. I sit there staring at her picture in a lot of disbelief, why someone so beautiful would want to lose all that weight and do this to one's self? Then it hits me that while the world was idolizing her for being so pretty, she herself was very unhappy with the way she looked.

Maybe my judgment of her is wrong to begin with. **Thin shaming** also crushes a person's self-esteem. She is entitled to lose as much weight as she wants to. **It's her body. It should be her decision.**

Not a Lesser Woman

6:30 am, after my Fajar prayers I grab my phone to check it, somehow we are so addicted to our phones it's the last thing we see before we shut our eyes and the first thing after we open them. Our phones have become a part of our existence; the addictive social media and its various features, and uncountable WhatsApp groups where random messages and bad jokes are forwarded. A few people in these groups are from the "religious clan", and to fulfill their religious duty, they bombard the group with religious forwards without checking the authenticity of the content. In some WhatsApp groups, you have common members, so the bad jokes are sent to your darling phone twice to chock the memory card. Last but not the least are the motivational messages (read blood boilers) that tell you to enjoy your Monday, Tuesday, Wednesday, Thursday, Friday, Saturday, and Sunday. They are sent to you free of cost, without fail, first thing in the morning.

I look at my phone and one such message appears:

"Good morning! Have a wonderful Wednesday. You are not behind. It's not too late. You're exactly where you're supposed to be. Everything is unfolding. Don't judge yourself or be hard on yourself about how long something is taking to happen. Your time is coming. Just be thankful you made it this far."

Okies - I think over and wonder, does she write this or is it copy and paste? Trying to understand the depth of the message, but my neurons are still asleep. For God's sake, it's 6:30 in the morning; I need caffeine, not a sermon.

I make French toast from bran bread for my kids, thinking it's so early in the morning they will not have the energy to argue with me and cry that the bread tastes bad. I pour a glass of hot water for myself with a spoon full of apple cider vinegar, some cinnamon, and a dash of raw organic honey - nothing less than a concoction, while keeping a close eye on the red *Prestige* frying pan so I don't burn the already brown toast.

Suddenly I hear screaming; upon listening closely, it becomes clear it's none other than Hamza, 'Mom! Mom! Come here!' I try to ignore his voice and hope that Ashoo would ask him what the issue is. I continue sipping my concoction for eternal fitness. Hamza yowls; I quickly take the toast off the stove and hurry towards his room where he is standing half-naked fighting with his uniform.

'MOM, *meray* uniform *mein kuch masla hai.*'

'Yes, of course, *masla hai*- It's not yours.'

I turn to the other one who has very conveniently worn a uniform shirt two sizes bigger than him and is brushing his hair.

Giving both of them a good doze early in the morning for being doped, I leave the room to hurry to the kitchen. Thinking it was a bad idea to put all the kids in the same school. My fitness concoction has gone absolutely cold and the purpose of drinking it warm, so it can cut all my fat, has absolutely been sabotaged by my offspring.

'Aaghhh! For these monkeys, I sacrificed my figure.' I muttered to myself, not that I was a size-zero, to begin with, but still, this added cushioning was not needed.

I spend most of my day running after them, till the time either of us is exhausted and goes to sleep. They say *"Not to fear childbirth, that's the easy part, there is no epidural for Motherhood"*. Sigh. I wonder why women voluntarily take up this position called **motherhood**. Going through the ordeal of pregnancy; the trauma of delivering a child, replacing their beautiful bodies with stretch marks and c-section scars. Is it because '*Heaven*' is under our feet or do we get a *GOD complex* out of it? Or is it society's norm to make womanhood complete? I often contemplate what sadistic joy we women get out of this entire ordeal. I mean, to procreate once is understandable, but to want to do this, again and again, requires a massive amount of insanity.

Exhausting my neurons all day about the torments and trials of motherhood and getting no gratifying answers, I proceed to change for the wedding in the family tonight.

I take out my taupe color kurta with silver and gold work on the sleeves, embellished by *gotta* and magenta piping. I match it with a silk fawn color trouser that Master *Sahib* has beautifully copied from the designer picture I showed him on my phone. He added golden seashells at the end of the trouser, proudly telling me that everyone will think it's from a boutique. To add color to the *kurta*, I pair it with beautiful peridot green and magenta color *chunnri*, heavily embellished with *kamdani* and *gotta*.

I carefully prepare my skin for makeup with a moisturizer and two primers. I mixed various foundations to achieve a flawless base with contouring for the cheeks and a chiseled jaw-line. I apply a heavy layer of concealer to camouflage the dark circles surrounding my beautiful hazel eyes.

I then adorn my eyes with a blend of *'Tease'* for the crease, and *'snakebite' and 'booty call'* for the corner and the lid. These are the erotic names of eye shadows in the Naked 2 palette that I use for my eyes. I add a dash of *smash box Vlada* shimmer drops on the lid to give it a soft glittery look. Cheeks brushed with *NARS super-Orgasm* blusher and *Benefit*'s dull-gold highlighter. To complete my look, I align my lips with Anastasia Beverly Hills' *dusty Lilac* lip color.

As I am wearing my *chaand baalies*, Ashoo walks over to the dresser and asks, 'Zo, how long will you take?' Absolutely ignoring the fact that I am looking marvelous and he is so lucky to have me in his life. I give him a look from the corner of my winged eye-liner and ask him, 'How do I look? 'Which actually means; it's time to give a nice compliment or else be ready for a fight. He quickly says "very nice" and summons that I should be in the car in 5 minutes.

"Very nice" I mean seriously? What does "very nice" mean? Why does he have such a limited vocabulary? Looking at the clock on my blue bedroom wall, I swiftly grab my glittery gold clutch and slip into the 7-inch golden shimmery heels that I got from Aldo. Quickly taking a selfie, I send it to Dina who immediately replies: "*Hotness*" along with the dancing girl emoji. I smile and flash to the car before World War III happens.

Upon reaching the venue of the event, we are welcomed by the *mami*s and *chachi*s of the bride. The other end of the garden has a beautiful marigold and fairy light stage, where both the bride and groom are sitting, looking super-cute and in love, getting their pictures taken.

I walk towards the center of the garden to meet people and spotted Zarina.

Zarina is my mom's first cousin's daughter, married to Ashoo's phupo's (paternal aunty) son. Instead of a family tree, we are actually a bush when it comes to marrying within the family.

Zarina walks towards me looking pretty; wearing a maroon color *kameez* with gold *dabka* work, black pants, and a golden *dupatta* with maroon and red paisleys' embroidery on it. Her hair is in a tight bun and ruby *jhumkas* are dangling from her ears.

'Assalam-o-Alaikum, Zoie, *baray dino kay baad mulaqaat hui* (Meeting you after ages). Before I could even reply to her greeting, she says, 'Zoie, *koi* good news *hai kya?*', bending her face towards my ear as if trying to whisper.

I look at her in shock, and with a confused face I say, '*Naaaaaahi.*'

'*Acha, mujhey laga* pregnant *ho.*' she is suddenly called by someone at a distance, and she leaves me standing there, feeling shocked, fuming, and miserable.

'What did she just ask me? Do I look pregnant in these clothes? Is she saying I am FAT but not in so many words?' These are the precise thoughts on my mind.

I had spent 45 minutes getting dressed to perfection, and this is what I get. I had asked Asher how I was looking, why didn't he tell me I looked pregnant in these clothes? How could he do this to me? He just said 'very nice'. Does 'very nice' mean you are looking

FAT? Otherwise, he would have said 'hot', 'pretty', or something romantic. OMG! Did he do it on purpose?

I am filled with rage and annoyance and ready to give Asher a piece of my mind when we get back in the car. I move towards a table in the corner so no one will see me, and no one will ask me if I was pregnant or not.

As I move closer to the table, I see Marium sitting with Fako *Khala* or Falknaz *Khala*, who is my late *Nani*'s cousin. She is technically *Amma*'s *khala* (aunt) but the whole *khandan* now calls her Fako*Khala*; what an entangled web our family is? We can never know who is related to whom. I offer my *salaam* to both. They seem busy in a conversation, so I sit a little away from them. Fako *Khala* asks me to come closer and sit next to her. She continues giving Marium some kind of advice, which Marium clearly is uncomfortable with.

Marium is also a second cousin from *Amma*'s side. She is a talented girl. A gold medalist from LUMS (Lahore University of Management Science), works for an MNC and is the most humble and down-to-earth person I have met in the family. She has no attitude about her success, super pretty and thin by *desi* standards. She married her class-fellow, Zain, from LUMS who is also a thorough gentleman. They have been married some 10 odd years.

Despite trying and going through various treatments and *totka*s, Marium and Zain have not been—hmm - as we call it "blessed" with a child yet. Regardless of all her achievements, Marium is always asked one question i.e. when she will have a kid? She has been offered free advice by practically everyone in the family, to go see XYZ doctor or fertility clinic. Today is also one of those sessions where Fako *Khala* has been giving her free advice and unasked information about a clinic where her neighbor's daughter went to, and now she has her *"Goud Bharie"* (literally means womb filled).

Marium is looking down and listening to the advice given to her. She seems upset and tired of the same topic that is brought in front of her again and again.

Fako *Khala* turns towards me and says, 'Zoie, *tum isko batao bachon kay baray mein, tumharay tou MashahAllah dou hain, mein zara sab sey mil kar aati hoon.*' She leaves us with an awkward silence.

Marium looks up with a dejected face. I am thinking of ways to change the topic, when she impulsively says, 'Zoie, how are the kids?'

'Fine, *Alhamdulillah.*' I reply carefully, weighing my words.

'They must be all grown-up now. You must be so happy now that the toddler days are over, less work for you.' She says innocently.

"Less work" I give some thought to her words. Yeah, right! They make me go crazy, you aren't missing much; I wanted to tell her, but instead, I smile in agreement.

An awkward silence, again. I want to ask her about her killer job and the corporate world, but before I could say a word, she comes out with a list of elucidation.

'Zoie, I have tried so many treatments, from hormonal medicines to fertility injections. Zain and I have made many *dua*s for a child too; it's not that we have not tried our best, but Allah has not listened to any of our prayers yet,' she says with a bit of complaint in her voice. 'We both have discussed the option of adopting a child, but Zain's mother does not agree.'

With sympathy in my eyes, I look at her in silence. She continues in a heartrending tone, 'You know Zoie, now I am just tired and fed up with this topic. Why can't people just leave me alone and not give me free advice for once?' She says with sorrow.

'I am so done with this "*Bacha kab hoga, abhi tak bachay nahi howay, bechari kay bachay nahi hain*" talk. I am so done with this.' She repeats, sounding more hurt.

'I don't need people's pitiful looks or medical counseling. I have seen enough doctors for a lifetime. ***Am I a lesser woman because I don't have children?*** She asks sounding sad.

Again an awkward silence stands between us. I have to say something to make her feel better, but words are not coming to me as easily as they usually do.

Then I just spar my heart out.

'No, Marium. You are not a lesser woman. You are a wonderful person. You are very well educated, have been successful professionally, all because of your hard work and talent, and have a loving partner. You are truly blessed with an intelligent mind and a kind heart.'

'See, the thing with us humans is that Allah has blessed us with so many things which we simply take for granted. We complain about that one thing HE hasn't blessed us with. Why he blesses some with children and some with not is HIS will. Why you, I cannot answer that Marium, but I know that if you surrender to HIS will, follow his *righteous path*. HE will bless you in ways you cannot fathom.'

'You must think it's easier for me to say that because I have been blessed with children, and perhaps you are right. I cannot know what you are feeling or going through. But I know that Allah has chosen you for something else. **HE only tests those whom HE loves the most.** Why Allah tests us despite loving us, I seriously don't know.'

Marium leans towards me and gave me a tight hug and says, 'Thank you, Zoie. This means a lot to me.'

I smile and hug her back. I wonder if I should ask her about my dressing, whether I am still that *Moti* Zoie from childhood or Zarina said it merely out of jealousy – huh!

'Marium, can I ask you something?' I ask her finally.

'Ya sure, Zoie.'

'Do I look healthy in these clothes?' I ask shyly.

'No! Of course not. In fact, your makeup looks stunning. You really have to teach me someday.'

'Sure! any day.' I say smiling and thinking she is a gold medalist from the top university in the country. Why would she lie?

'Come on, Marium, food is served, let's eat.' She smiles in agreement.

I drive back home thinking about my conversation with Marium. After all that, I feel less angry towards Ashoo, rather I feel ashamed; how often have I been ungrateful for the blessings given by Allah? How often I have questioned HIS wisdom. Today at the same event I was upset because someone called me pregnant, and she was upset because she is unable to get pregnant. This is the reality of this world. The heart desires what it sees. The mind may understand, but it's the heart that never listens.

I lay in bed that night thinking about our society and how constantly women are judged by other women. A woman's body is not worthy enough if she can't reproduce; what kind of twisted body-shaming is this? I kept thinking about Marium, how patiently she listens to unsolicited advice from people who have no medical background. How she is continuously under the pressure of trying to please the Creator because the society perceives her to be cursed. How she will answer personal questions for the rest of her life or until she is "blessed" according to the societal standards.

As a society, how often we enter people's personal domain, not realizing that we are not helping. Sometimes it's best to be quiet than to say something so hurtful that would make someone feel uncomfortable in their own skin. There should be limits for jokes and asking private questions. **There should be 'limits' for giving advice that is not welcomed or needed. How often we cross our limits we don't even know.**

Heavy Bag Weight Loss: Depending on your weight and overall level of fitness, boxing can be an extremely effective means of burning calories and toning muscle fiber. A 155-pound person punching a bag can burn around 422 calories per hour. (Google fact)

My knuckles HURT

The next morning, I get up angry and go straight to the gym. After being called pregnant, I have to do something about the *muffin top* that had found refuge on my stomach.

Weights, lunges, jumping jacks, planks, my favorite squat & hold, and finally a round of boxing, punching the bag till my knuckles hurt; I seriously took umbrage of the remarks made by Zarina.

My darling trainer gives me an admirable look: 'You worked very hard today, Zoie.' She says with pride in her voice.

Upon reaching home, I write a long message to Dina and tell her all about what Zarina had said to me last night.

To the half-page message that I wrote narrating my sad saga about the night, Dina replies, 'What a B-I-T-C-H (in Urdu). Why didn't you give her hell?'

'I should have, Dina, maybe next time when I see her, I will,' is my reply.

I quickly send the same message about B-I-T-C-H (in Urdu) Zarina to the WhatsApp **sisters** group. Anu is busy with the baby so she sends me an angry face emoji. And Aambi *Appa* is probably sleeping because of the time difference between our continents.

I then call *Amma* and tell her about what her cousin's daughter had said to me. To which *Amma* inquires, 'Are you pregnant, Zoie?'

'*Amma*! Please! NO!!' I reply with frustration in my voice.

'*Chalo agar uss ney keh diya koi baat nahi.*' She says.

'Zoie, you should have asked her how she is so fit after having 4 kids.'

'Zoie! Leave *roti*, *chaawal*, *aloo*, and *meetha*. Just leave all these things *beta*,' is her unasked advice cum diet plan to me which I have been hearing all my life.

I put the phone down, thinking; it's no use calling *Amma*. She never takes my side.

<u>Part two:</u>

"Thirty-five is a very attractive
age. London society is full of women
of the very highest birth
who have, of their own free choice,
remained thirty-five for years."

- Oscar Wilde

ZOIE turns 40!

2nd September

At midnight, Ashoo and the kids enter the room holding a cake full of candles and two boxes wrapped neatly in pink and white floral wrapping paper. I am pretending to be asleep so I won't spoil the surprise for them. The approximately 2lbs cake is coated in buttercream cheese icing with caramel swirls all over the top; a perfect *Salted Caramel* flavor with *"Happy 40th"* written on it with green icing.

My phone kept buzzing with notifications from Dina, Anu, my in-laws, and a few other friends. After the singing and group hugs, I cut the cake. Muhammad and Hamza hand me the bigger box out of the two boxes that are now placed on my bed. Inside the box was a beautiful Sage colored *Kurta* from Koel with gold and black paisleys block-printed all over it. The neck-line is embellished with sage color buttons; simple and elegant. I quickly check the size; Size 12. Well! I am working out so much a 10 size would fit me easily. I will have to change it tomorrow.

The smaller box is from Ashoo. Inside the box is a beautiful bangle with a *swan* in the center. The *magnificent swan* is studded with white crystals and a silver sterling rim that covers the entire wrist. It's just beautiful. I don't know why swans are my favorite birds. Maybe the fairytale of the ugly duckling that turns into a beautiful swan is entrenched deep in my subconscious.

After a session of the cake followed by some lemongrass tea to burn the calories, we finally call it a night.

I spend the next morning replying to the birthday wishes on various social media forums. The first message that I reply to was from Saim.

Saim and I have been friends since college, till he flew to the US to complete his degree program. We lost touch after he left, but thanks to Facebook we reconnected and stayed in touch. I am his therapist in times of stress, at least that's what he calls me. We often have long discussions on politics and the cultural norms of the society.

Saim has had a difficult teenage. He was a late bloomer, extremely thin, with a lot of acne scars on his face. He was exceptionally intelligent but shy. He could never get much female attention in his younger days. As a grown man, he opted for an arranged marriage which sadly didn't work for him either. It ended in an ugly divorce followed by depression and low self-esteem.

Heartbroken and depressed, he could not muster the courage to marry again. Doesn't say it out loud, but I feel somewhere deep down he is badly hurt.

His messages are simple and to the point, and today is also no exception.

'Happy Birthday, Zoie. So how old are u now??????' He has written with many question marks.

'Thank you, Saim.*sigh* 40 but I feel 29.' I quickly write back.

'Ha ha, ya right. You are older to me; I will turn 40 in December.' He replies with a wink emoji.

'So, what's new Saim?' I quickly want to change the subject; my age is something I don't want to talk about.

'Reading a very interesting book called *Breaking Curfew*, it talks about various aspects of life in Pakistan, like politics, religion, bureaucracy, and the army. The book is so informative. I mean, the amount of unabashed corruption in this Land of the pure is mind-blowing."

'Land of the pure, Saim, is a cliché.'

'You must read this book, Zoie. Those chick-lit you read are worthless.'

'That's not true. I read other stuff too, but I have a fetish for chick-lits. They put one's mind in a cheerful place. You should read it too sometime.'

'I have given up on romance a long time ago, you know that.'

'Why Saim? There are a lot of fish in the sea; you just have to keep your hooks sharp. Who knows you will be lucky the second time.'

'I will keep that in mind, Zoie. Okay, got to go. Have a rocking day, will catch u later.'

'Thanks, Saim, take care.'

I end my text with a happy-face emoji, thinking what is he waiting for; men in this country marry left, right and center, and he has taken one poor relationship to his heart. Saim has confided in me that his depression had gotten terrible a few months after his divorce, for which he started taking antidepressants. A side-effect of the medicines was that he had gained a lot of weight. To avoid questions and body shaming jokes, he had stopped meeting people. I was among a few people he would message when he needed some venting out. We never discussed his depression after that day.

Maybe I will convince Saim to join a yoga class, I think. I mean, men do yoga all over the world; it's not only for women. Such crazy taboos we have in this country. Men will only do gym and weights to look manly. We have silly standards of macho-ism. I need to use my matchmaking skills for Saim, for sure, I think while replying to the birthday wishes from all my single female friends. And mentally short-listing a few for Saim.

♣

Later in the day, Dina and Anu have organized a birthday party for me at Anu's place. I rush to my regular salon for a nice and relaxing session of manicure/pedicure followed by an outward blow dry. Hurry back home to wear a black and gold vertical striped top (vertical lines make you look thinner)with black boot cut pants, give extra detailing to the makeup today to create a perfect no-makeup look. I wonder why it is called a no-makeup look. There is a lot of makeup used to create that so-called natural look. I mean, seriously, nobody wakes up looking like this for sure.

Anu and Dina have surely outdone themselves decorating the house with black and gold balloons and tea light candles. The cake was amazing; a super, two-tier, mocha chocolate cake with the letters'4' and '0' placed on top surrounded with buttercream icing flowers in pink and yellow. The food was delicious; chicken sandwiches, khowsey, a large bowl of rocket and avocado salad, and some mouth-watering *Pani Puri.*

To my surprise, they both have invited a lot of women from my circle of people, from old school-friends to new mom-friends. *Amma* was also there; she is so happy to see the setup, Aambi *Apa* also joins us via a video call.

The air is buzzing with laughter, the smell of yummy food, and a sense of happiness. Pictures and selfies are being taken with the *birthday GIRL*, gifts are being opened. Later in the evening, Ashoo and the kids join us, too. We reach home happily exhausted. The evening ends with Ashoo and I sneaking out for some ice-cream once the kids go to sleep.

♣

The next morning I wake up happy until pictures of last evening's party are shared. And that makes me go under utter shock. Oh my God! Is it me? I look so bloated in these pictures - is my first reaction. Who took this full-length picture with my butt sticking out? Why am I looking so dark in this picture, my chin is so obvious? Why can't people just crop my face and then post the picture? These are a few among the many anxiety-filled reactions I have.

They say the camera adds 10 pounds to your normal self, REALLY! I kept scrolling the pictures in distress.

Maybe I should have confiscated everyone's cell phones. I should have only asked Anu to take pictures and apply those beauty filters to each picture before they were posted for the world to see. Oh, God! These bloated pictures will remain in **"The Cloud"** forever.

Deadly DETOX

4th September.... Two days later.

I try wearing the *Kurta* that Ashoo and the kids gave me for my birthday. It is somehow a bit tight. Looking in the mirror I try to suck in my stomach but it still shows the tiers of my waistline, pretty much like the two-tier cake I had gobbled down my throat.

I stand in front of the mirror, trying to figure out what to do. I shortlist my options: should I take it back to the shop and get a bigger size? I couldn't have possibly gained weight. I have been killing myself at the gym, the size must have dropped by now. Is it bloating due to that time of the month? I have been eating cake for the past two days. Is it the damn cake?

Guilt takes over me. 6 months have passed since I decided to get a body like Amir Khan, and now I am not even fitting in a *Kurta*. Why does it always happen to me? I suddenly drown in self-loathing.

Desperate times call for desperate measures. I decide to immediately detox my body for the next 7 days and then go on a soup diet for the rest of the month. Maybe I should join a yoga class in the evening so my body can stretch and loosen up. I checked the archive of my email. Anu had recently shared a very nice detox recipe given by an A-list nutritionist who lives in Dubai and is very popular among the ladies of K-town.

The email read:

Deadly Detox: a seven-day plan to rid the body of all the toxins

Start your day with 1-liter hot water with lemon 30 mins later, have a banana + 1 bowl of watermelon with 1 tbsp of flax seeds and 1 tsp of pumpkin seeds, chia seeds, and sesame seeds

Midday Snack:

A handful of nuts + 2 dates along with 1 liter of hot water with lemon and a cup of freshly brewed chamomile tea.

Lunch:

2 bananas + 1 bowl of pineapple and one cup freshly brewed lemongrass tea

Evening Snack:

Half avocados with lemon juice and chilies + 1 liter of hot water with lemon

Dinner:

Watermelon + my signature cabbage and pumpkin soup recipe

Before bedtime

1 cup of coconut milk with ½ tsp of freshly ground turmeric + 1 tsp raw organic honey with cinnamon powder.

Guaranteed results in 7 days.

I spend the rest of my day in searching for the ingredients for my deadly detox. I check three stores for avocados only to find out they were Rs. 595/- per piece. No luck finding pumpkin seeds. The local supermarket doesn't carry "*kadoo kay beej*".

Instead of doing 7 days, I end my detox after four days of going to the bathroom every 5 minutes. Those four days were so good, I was focused and dedicated; with a bit of cheating (*3 spoons of biryani, two bites of chicken and some chips, but that doesn't count, at least I am going to the gym regularly*).

'Hunger is the first element of self-discipline. If you can control what you eat and drink, you can control everything else.'

5 Stages of DIETING

After a somewhat successful detox session, I decide to go absolutely cold turkey on my diet. We, women, have been dieting practically all our lives. We are born dieters, it's in our DNA to sacrifice our 'various' cravings. Women all over the world are doing it, so can't I?

Day1: Time to get healthy. At 8:30 am, Ashoo is at the table reading the newspaper, I take out the Greek yogurt and blueberries from the fridge, pour the yogurt in an empty bowl carefully measuring it with a measuring cup, I then quickly grab the bag of organic granola that I had just bought last night and sprinkle it over the yogurt carefully taking a palm-size helping; they say your palm is your measuring cup because your stomach is the size of your palm. Really! I wonder who are those people who only eat palm-sized meals, my meals are my palm-size multiplied by 5, and that too when I am on a diet. Okay, coming back to my diet-bowl, I then carefully decorate the blueberries and half-sliced banana on the corners of the bowl and sprinkle some sesame seeds on top. Wow! What a perfect and healthy bowl, but I must take a picture for my Instagram before I indulge in this hale and hearty meal. Before I could take a bite, Ashoo asks me what I was eating, I tell him it's a 'granola breakfast bowl', healthy for the stomach and heavy on the pocket. The prices of these imported goods have increased so much. Though, being a *pakka pakka* supporter of Khan *Sahab*, I am also very upset with this increase in prices. Khan *Sahab*, in his address to the *awaam*, has asked us to go local. What can I do if blueberries are not produced locally; is it my fault? The new policies are sucking the blood out of the already existing filers. And talking about locally produced stuff, their prices have skyrocketed, too. I think Khan *Sahab* wants the nation to be fit; no one will eat anything because the prices are so high and everyone will be fit and smart; this seems to be his actual plan. In *Naya* Pakistan, we all will be thin and poor.

Day2: I begin my day with a healthy régime of hot water and lemon and spend the rest of my day carefully choosing healthy stuff. To satisfy my craving for candy, I chose nature's candy called 'fruits', that too the juicy, high fiber ones, being proud of myself for showing such resilience on my second day.

Day3: Clear soup and salad; I realize there is not much one can do with a salad to make it taste different. No matter what you add, it will always taste like salad.

Day4: My neighbor invites me for tea at her place; since it's been ages we met, I decided to go and meet her and get *sawab* (reward) for "*Huqooq-e-Paros*". Upon reaching her house, I am surprised to meet other aunties of the neighborhood. Sadia, my neighbor, has set up a beautiful table for tea, with goodies ranging from our regular chaat-samosa to pasta and salad. I spot the beautiful salad bowl in the center of the table with different green vegetables in it. Perfect for my diet, I think. Taking out a spoonful in my plate, I notice fried-chicken popcorns inside the salad; the greens had a thick white layer of mayonnaise coating them. I stare at my plate thinking what to do; the other stuff on the table is either fried or rich in carbs. I look around; the ladies of the neighborhood are chit-chatting and enjoying the snacks. *How are they all eating this stuff* is the first thought in my mind? Shouldn't they be worried about their health, like me? Having no other choice, I take a bite of the salad that I have poured on my plate. To my surprise it tastes good, the chunky fried chicken is giving a bit of a crunch to the salad; the sweetness of the cold mayonnaise makes it taste more like a dessert. I gobble it down my throat, thinking - it's still salad.

Same Day: As I finish my salad and I am about to keep my plate back on the table, Sadia brings piping hot *fried* Jalapeno poppers from the kitchen.

'Zoie, you must try these, I made them fresh today.' She says with culinary pride.

The Jalapenos look so good and I don't want to be rude to my neighbor by saying that I don't eat all this stuff. After all, there is something known as courtesy.

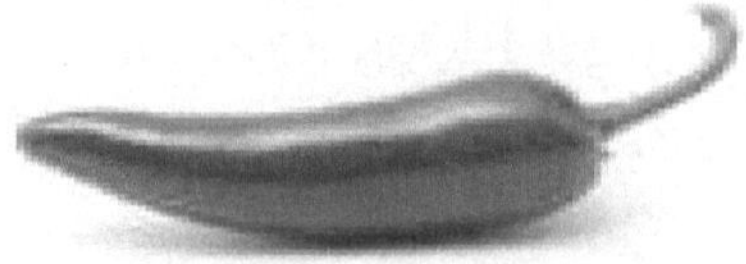

I pick the hot jalapeno and place it on my plate. Sadia stands next to me waiting for me to take a bite, so I can give my feedback on her cookery skills. Under immense pressure by my host, I take a small bite of the delicacy. The crispy breadcrumb quoting and the soft melted cheese was absolutely to die for. With *hmm* and *yum* sounds, I finish the entire popper thinking and convincing myself; *Jalapeno is a vegetable.*

After gorging on the jalapeno, the aftermath of the slight sharpness of the chili is making my taste buds burn a bit. I look around the table and spot pasta. Should I or shouldn't I? I stand there thinking *is pasta carbs too??*

Day 5: Maybe I am being too hard on myself. The weekend is around the corner and no one diets on weekend, after all, we live for the weekend. Okay, by Monday I will start my diet again. *Pakka* promise!

Behind every couple, there is a

Mother-in-law.

Sin Tax

A week later....

On Thursday, around midday, I reach my editor's office in an old dilapidated and the grimiest building in Karachi. The staircase is abstractly painted with spits from *Paan* and *Gutka*. I climb up the stairs, ignoring the elevator, and reach the office on the third floor. A bit of cardio for the body during the day is very essential, plus I don't want to risk my life by getting in the elevator that looks like a grade 5 science-project of *Otis* (may *Elisha Otis'* soul rest in peace). Upon reaching the office, I notice a sad *Pathan Laala* sitting at the entrance. Everyone calls him *Pathan Laala* as no one knows his actual name. He is the peon cum delivery boy cum telephone operator at the office; he is the only cheerful person in this workplace and greets everyone with a lot of energy, but today he is sitting in the corner on his broken wooden stool with sadness in his eyes.

'Salaam, *Laala. Kya howa, aaj udaas ho, sub khairiyat?*' I ask while entering the office.

'*Kya bataoon baji, bas deera pareeshani da,*' is his reply.

I give him a questionable look; to which he replies:

'*Baji, pehlay* naswaar (a form of tobacco) 10 *rupay ka tha, ab* **tax** *lag gaya hai us per ek* packet 15 *rupay ka hogaya hai. Aap batao ghareeb aadmi kya karay, naswaar bhi nahi khaye tou kesay jeeye.*' He says looking glum.

I can feel the pain in his heart. I mean, I am a Khan *Sahab*'s supporter, but this *naswaar pey* tax is way out of line. On the other hand, the reason for *Pathan-laala*'s sheer *'joie de vivre'* is because he is always high. Maybe we all should try it once in a while since the economic condition doesn't seem to get better any sooner, but it will, Khan *Sahab* has promised and told us repeatedly, *'ghabrana nahi hai'*.

With empathy, I silently nod in agreement and move towards my editor's office. The reason for my visit today is to discuss my new assignment, but the actual reason is, I want to collect the cheques for the work I had done previously.

My always-busy editor is talking on the phone, leaning on his chair and his reading-glasses are placed on the tip of his nose, he asks me to take a seat by pointing his finger towards the chair while he continues with his telephonic conversation. I sit at the edge of the chair thinking about the germs and contamination public chairs carry. At that very moment my cell phone rings, I take it out from my purse, and the screen flashes "Mom-in-Law", instantly my first thought is to cancel the call as her phone calls, like my mom, are never short and I am at work, but canceling her call means she will immediately call her son telling him that she called me and I didn't answer her phone. To avoid any domestic repercussions, I glance at my editor, who is still busy on his phone, and quietly step out of his room to pick up the most important call.

'Hello Aunty *Assalam-o-Alaikum.*' I say immediately, answering the phone.

'*Wa-alaikum* Zoie *beta, kab sey* phone *kar rahie hoon, ghar pey bhe kiya tou Sughra nay bataya subha sey bahar gaie ho, kahan ho beta?*' Is her long reply.

Without giving her many details, I reply by saying '*Kaam sey nikli hoon* aunty, *aap bataiye koi kaam hai?*'

'*Haan beta,aaj raat ka khana yaheen khana tum sab, mein ney Nihari banai hai, Ashoo, Hamza aur Muhammad ko pasand hai na*(please note that my name is not in the list), bas *Shazia bhi aa rahi hai* family *kay sath, tum log* time *sey pohonch jana, theek hai?*' (Shazia is my sister-in-law)

Having no other choice, I say, '*Jee* aunty.'

'*Beta Zoie kitni baar kaha hai mujhey* mama *kaha karo, tum phir bhi* aunty *kehti ho, itnay saal hogaye tumhari shaadi ko.*' Is her complain cum order.

'*Jee aunty, oops sorry mama.*'

We reach her house at 8:00 PM sharp; she has already set up the table. Upon seeing us enter the house, she warmly hugs her two grandchildren, Hamza and Muhammad, and then she moves towards me to hug me and Ashoo. After some chit-chat with Shazia and others, we eat dinner; a meaty gastronomic cuisine for the entire family. I notice how Ashoo, like a little boy, is excited to see his mom's home-cooked meal, I turn towards my two offspring who are ready to stuff their faces with Nihari. I look around the table, thinking I should say goodbye to my diet. At that very moment, my mom-in-law walks out of the kitchen holding a bowl of salad, she comes towards me, 'Zoie, *yeh try karo* new recipe *sey* salad *banai hai*, morning show *mein dekhi thiee* recipe.'

I look at the bowl to find a nicely diced salad with cucumbers, broccoli, and juicy cherry tomatoes

'Zoie, lemon *aur* olive oil *ki* dressing *hai iss mein, tumhain pasand hai na.*'

With admiration in my eyes, I take out two spoonfuls in my plate, thinking how lucky I am to have such a wonderful woman like her in my life. I should be thankful to her for raising Ashoo so well, maybe I should leave my two monsters with her too, so she can discipline them and nurture them with love. Since she does not have a Wi-Fi in her house, it would be a blessing to not have the kids engrossed in their gadgets for once.

She has baked some chicken for my father-in-law; he is a diabetic and can't eat such gourmet cuisines. She asks me to try the chicken, which is super tender; it has fulfilled my intake of proteins.

I stand there thinking about the word 'mom', how this one word has the feeling of ownership attached to it, all moms- be it mom or mom-in-law - want to own their kids because of the immense love they hold in their heart.

I take the last bite of my salad and move towards the table where my mom-in-law is standing. I want to thank her for the yummy and healthy meal she made for all of us, but even before I could utter a word she says, 'Zoie *sahi sey khaya beta? Waisay thora ziada khaana khaya karo, aagey aur bachay kaisay paida karo gi? Ab* Muhmmad 5 *saal ka hogaya hai, ab iska bhai ya behan aana chaheye.'*

I stand there looking at her in absolute shock; it is taking me forever to get rid of the pregnancy weight from when Muhammad was born, and now she is making secret plans to sabotage all my efforts with her bizarre ideas, just when I started liking her she had to become a typical mom-in-law. *UFFF*!!!

Culture stereotypes women to fit the myth by flattening the feminine into beauty-without-intelligence or intelligence-without-beauty; women are allowed a mind or a body, but NOT both.

(Naomi Wolf)

The Invitation

Mid-September...... heat at its peak.

At 9:00 in the morning, I receive 3 WhatsApp notifications; one from an unknown number, 2nd from Dina and one video shared in the school moms' group. I quickly open the unknown number chat, to my surprise it's an invitation to our annual reunion party. After graduating, I have only attended one reunion so far. Every year something comes up and I end up missing the party, thinking I will go next year.

Then I check Dina's messages; she has asked me if I have received the invite and whether or not I plan to go. Instinctively, I write 'yes, I will go' to which Dina suggested that we should go together. The next message is obviously about what we will wear and that we both have nothing in our closets, so we need to go shopping.

Exactly a month and a half to the reunion, I better lose some **more** weight, I ponder. I visualize all the successful people from my batch that will be at the reunion. They surely can't see me with all this weight. I will go on a very strict diet for five weeks straight to look presentable at the reunion. Also, I need to buy clothes in black color, the only slimming color in the world.

Later in the week, I step out to order something for Jibbo's wedding, which is just 3 months away. I pay Mehr a visit. Mehr is a talented designer who works from home. She is a mother of three cute 'triplets' yet she did not give up work. Doing all her work at home is the way she can be with her triplets and simultaneously follow her passion for designing beautiful clothes.

Upon reaching her house, I am guided by one of her staff members to wait for Mehr in her studio. I can't help but admire how tastefully Mehr has converted one room in her house into a beautiful working studio. The three walls are painted in nude peachy tones, and the back wall of her studio has the most beautiful abstract wallpaper in shades of brown. The center of the room has a long chandelier that almost rubs the ground, reminding me of a set from an Ashwariya Rai's movie. The extreme end of the room has a working desk and two chairs. I breeze through the designs' booklet that is kept on the desk, choosing a rich teal-green shirt with maroon pants for Jibbo's wedding.

I am offered tea by the most cordial of her staff members, informing me that she will see me as soon as she is free; she is busy explaining the patterns to her workers. I so admire such women who show courage and zeal to do something in life. Also, Mehr is among those very few designers who don't mention your weight while taking order; she tactfully designs around it, giving subtle suggestions.

A petite and dusky looking Mehr enters the room with her luscious, curly hair parted from the center.

'Hello, Zoie.' She moves forward to hug me.

'You look so good, seems you have been working out.'

A sudden bubble of happiness catches and trickles into me. I feel so overjoyed to hear this; nobody has said that to me, although I have been grueling myself in the gym. Thank God for good Samaritans like Mehr, this world is a better place.

'Yes Mehr, I have been working out, but how can you tell?' I reply, curiously.

'Oh Zoie, I can tell. I make your clothes and I can spot a size change in a jiffy.'

With an ear-to-ear grin, I blush like a teenager who has just received a compliment.

'Zoie, what can I do for you?' Mehr asks in a professional tone.

I show her the design from one of her booklets; she suggests a few changes in color and design. She also shows me a few fabric options, asks me what my estimate of expense is, and finally, we agreed on something. It is in between what I want and what she could make in my budget.

As I am about to leave, Mehr suggests that she will do my final measurements just before the wedding, so if there is a further size change that can be easily fixed.

I smile and think, '*of course there will be a change. I am eating seeds and ghee and juicy green leaves. If there is no change now, then when.*'

Happy and elated, I stopped at the nearest mall for a bit and check out something for the annual reunion. Somehow, today, everything was going in my favor, which is so rare in my case. I notice a lovely black poncho with silver beaded sleeves in my size, and the fit was amazing. This day could not get any better, I muse happily and quickly buy the dress. In my jubilant mood, I loitered around the Mall, thinking Dina will kill me when I tell her I went to the Mall without her and bought something for the reunion. While passing by the shops, a certain smell catches my attention. It is the aroma of something being baked. I can't figure out what it is, but my nose is forcing me to follow that particular direction, just like a puppet whose strings are pulled by its marionette. In my case, the marionette is my nose that has taken over my other senses.

I walk towards where my nose is leading me; I find myself standing in front of a shop called *Baskin &Robbins*. The tantalizing aroma is that of freshly baked waffle cones. I stand under the cosmic sign that read BR in pink and blue.

Instinctively, I want to go inside and cheat. One scoop of waffle cone will not hurt me, or will it, are my thoughts. I mean, how many calories can it be? One small scoop and a petite waffle cone; I will not take any topping, I promise myself. I quickly check Google for net calories and in one scoop of ice-cream, to my surprise it is just 160 calories. The nutritional chart on the website of *Baskin&*

Robins also mentions the calcium, vitamin A&C details in one scoop.

'Ice-cream is a source of calcium, and calcium is good for the bones. After 40 you got to worry about those bones, right?' I ponder.

It is a simple calculation. The waffle cone is another 121 calories. So, 160 plus 121 is 281 calories. That's not much, or is it?

Struggling against the temptation of it, I cannot decide whether I should satisfy my urge for a quick sugar rush or to walk by BR and commit myself to my weight loss regime. I stand in front of the shop, confused. Then it hits me, I can go inside and ask for a few free taste samples of my favorite flavor. This way I will get instant gratification and dopamine will be released in my body to put me in a jovial kind of high. We all know that it's all in the mind. When a person eats sugar, the brain produces huge surges of dopamine, which in simple language is a happy hormone, and who doesn't want to be happy? A tiny bit of ice-cream to satisfy the taste buds, minus the 281 calorie guilt, that will lurk on for days and the cellulite that will find safe haven on the gluts, forever. Surely, *fat lasts longer than flavor.*

Thinking I have a master plan, I walk inside the shop and ask the person behind the chiller to give me a sample of my favorite *"old fashion butter pecan"*. The sample he hands over seems smaller than I had imagined, but I can always try other flavors.

As I put the spoon in my mouth, a state of delight takes over all my senses, putting me in a serene frame of mind. Swallowing my bite of what seems like a forbidden fruit in fitness-heaven, in that very moment I am interrupted by a familiar voice calling out my name.

I turn around with the spoon still in my mouth, and to my complete shock, it's none other than 'Zarina'.

There stands Zarina just behind me, wearing a peachy pink short *Kurti* and fitted jeans and a Burberry (read fake Burberry) scarf around her neck. Her hair are straight, mid-waist, parted from the side with sunshades resting on her head. I can't help but notice how thin her legs are. I recall the latest memory of her meeting me at a family wedding; she had called me pregnant, for which I am still a bit upset.

"Zoie, I saw you going inside the ice-cream shop, thought I must follow you and say hello."

They say it's a small world, yet I never bump into Ahad Raza Mir or Fawad Khan. I always bump into people like Zarina.

Like always, Zarina hardly gives me a chance to answer back and goes on and on.

'*Wah*, Zoie, shopping, and ice-cream? *Ayaashi hai,*' is her next cynical comment.

I smile back taking the spoon out of my mouth, and suddenly the taste of the butter pecan ice cream has turned muddy, I swallow it with effort, so I can make small-talk with her.

'So Zarina, what are you up to?' I ask trying to be polite.

'Oh you know, shopping; *Ammi* wants me to buy some lawn outfits for her.'

'Oh that's lovely, how is your mother?' I ask, sounding concern.

'No, Zoie, not my mom, it's my mother-in-law, *Ammmi*,' she says emphasizing the word, 'She so depends on me, only wears what I buy and I am responsible for the entire house now. She likes my choice of clothes.'

'See, it's a lot of responsibility living with your in-laws, one has to take care of so many things and moods. You *tou* live independent *na*, no responsibility on you.'

What? What did she just say, of course, I have responsibilities, and living on your own doesn't mean I don't have responsibilities. Dumbfounded I give her a questionable glance.

'Zoie my brother-in-law got engaged *na*, we are having an engagement party next month, will send invites soon, you must come.'

'Oh! Congratulations, so who is the lucky girl?' I ask.

'She works in his office, not from the family like us, an outsider and she is not even from our community,'. Her reply is accompanied by disapproval on her face.

'You mean they both work together, how lovely.' is my instant reply.

'What lovely *yaar*? *Ammi* is not happy with this *rishta*, plus the girl is a bit *moti*, she looks so much older than my brother-in-law.' is her judgmental reply.

'I am sure they both have a good understanding, Zarina.'

'Don't know *yaar*, *Ammi* wanted a daughter-in-law just like me, she even asked me to look for a girl just like me, but *aaj kal kay* boys, they don't listen.'

'*Chalo*, I have to go. I ordered Super Green juice, it must be ready by now and I have to pick it up from the food court. I *tou* eat nothing in the afternoon. Just green vegetable juice. After all, I have to maintain myself. I told you I take Zumba classes *na.*'

No, she never told me this, but I choose not to interrupt her.

'Zoie, you also switch to vegetable juice for weight loss, do Zumba, it really helps. I drink juice and don't feel hungry at all. You should try it, do some walk at least. And leave all this sugary stuff.' She says pointing to the empty pink spoon in my hand, which I had completely forgotten about.

I so want to show her the *middle finger,* but my own *Amma*'s fear stops me from doing so. I just forcibly smile back.

After a few seconds, she says goodbye and leaves. I feel a certain rage and remorse inside my heart, followed by a million questions. Did I ask her for fitness advice? No, but she still insisted on giving it to me; and Zumba? Seriously, who does Zumba now, dancing on suggestive Bollywood songs is so not fitness. And what did she mean by *walk, at least*? Why did she assume that I don't exercise? I do proper exercise, and yes I like to eat too, crucify me for eating.

Dina had given Zarina a perfect name B-I-T-C-H (in Urdu). She is so full of herself, self-centered narcissist. And why does her mother-in-law want another one like her? Isn't one e-n-o-u-g-h? I feel sad for the poor girl who will be a part of this family soon. She will never be good enough for the family with *"Miss Perfect"* around. Women marry all kinds of men; dark, fat, old, even bald, but we expect a man to marry a perfect Barbie doll. I can't imagine the gossip that will start in the family once they attend the engagement, all commenting on that poor bride's weight. She will receive fitness advice all her life. And God forbids, if she has a pigmented skin, according to *desi* standards, then that will be discussed along with her nose, eyes, and all her features. Women go through the worst body scrutiny and shaming in our culture. With one daughter-in-law skinny, there will be comparisons for the new bride all her life.

Here's how it is: I feel guilty about every single bite of food that goes into my mouth.

- Marian Keyes

The Curse

The next day, I reach half an hour early for my workout session. Thinking I need to put in more effort, at least for the coming weeks, to look good for the annual reunion. I have consumed a liter of scalding water with lemon early in the morning, and my bladder is working with supersonic speed. The workout is uncomfortable, as holding the bladder and exercising needed a lot more effort.

A woman's body is cursed; PCO, hormonal imbalance, thyroid issues, cellulite deposits, bloating, pre-menstrual water retention, pre-pregnancy weight, post-pregnancy weight, sagging skin, fibroids, cysts, and the list goes on. Men burn calories while watching Netflix.

Many women struggle, starve, and workout like crazy to drop a few pounds. Men take the stairs instead of an elevator and are in shape. Among the many inequalities of gender that exist in this universe, this is by far the most unjust.

The rest of my morning goes well; I take one boiled egg and green tea for breakfast, an apple as a mid-morning snack. Though I dipped my apple slices in peanut butter. Yum!! A heavenly taste. Whoever invented peanut butter should be eternally blessed. I have promised myself to switch to homemade organic butter after this bottle finishes.

We, women, are a bit of a masochist when it comes to enjoying food. We continuously count the calories we put in our respective mouths. Our calorie-intake is directly proportional to the amount of self- loathing we do each day. Every day, we count the number of calories we consume, so we can decide how much self-hate we can do that day. Sometimes it's mentally exhausting to feel guilty about every single bite we put in our mouth.

Trapped in this vicious circle of weight-loss and with little time left for the annual reunion, I need to only eat salad and drink lemon water to get in shape and look smashing for the party. It doesn't seem that difficult. After these weeks are over, I will continue eating salad and drinking lemon water until Jibbo's wedding. *Bas*!! I have decided to have self-control and promised myself that I will not cheat.

♣

Later in the day, Saim messaged me with a business proposal. I call him instead, and after the exchange of a few formal greetings, he comes straight to the point.

'Hey, Zoie, I was thinking that while you are hunting for a real job and working on your husband (for migration, to greener pastures), he said in a cynical tone, how about we start a website of something of interest like products of the northern areas of Pakistan, or *Desi* recipes? I don't know yet, but something interesting.'

'What do you have in mind Saim, and by the way, writing is an actual job?' I replied, rolling my eyes.

'Zoie, I have been thinking about it, the basic business model of a website or a blog, initially we will run it free of cost and once we have generated enough 'likes' and interest, we can charge money. Blogging is the new trend these days.'

Saim's enthusiasm has taken me by surprise.

'Or we could do counseling; highest paid jobs in the USA.' I say, quickly thinking of something.

'I know; they make so much money. Okay, Zoie, let's brainstorm ideas, we can have two or three websites and even if we make 1500 dollars a month, that's not bad for a side-business given the exchange rate. This idea came to me in my dream early this morning and I could not sleep since then, was waiting for dawn so I can message you.'

'Saim, let me brainstorm a few more ideas and do a bit of research, then we can have another discussion soon.'

'Yeah, sure take your time. So what's up?'

'Saim, did you get the invite for the reunion, are you going?' I ask anxiously.

He sighs, 'You know Zoie, I am not at ease meeting people. I can't answer so many questions about my life. Also, I have gained so much weight, I don't feel comfortable with public appearances, my size is always the first question people ask about me, plus you know what a mess my personal life is.' He says in a sad tone.

'Oh, come on Saim, it will be a pleasant change for you. Please come, *na*. Dina and I are going.' I reply with much excitement.

'I will feel uncomfortable and down in the dumps once I see a pool of successful people with their perfect lives as if social media was not enough to make me feel crappy about myself. Now meeting them in person, no Zoie I don't want to.'

'SAIM, please *yaar chalo*. Dina and I will be with you, it will be fun.' I am being extra careful not to use the word *depression* in this conversation.

'I will think about it, Zoie. But for now, I am planning to step out of this city and take 4 days off, and guess where I plan to go?' He intelligently changed the topic.

'Where are you going, Saim?' I ask, sounding surprised.

'Your favorite place; home away from home— *DUBAI.*'

'Oh wow! Now I am so jealous. When do you leave?'

'In two days, I will stay at the Hyatt Regency. I have booked it online; it's through a tour operator, which solves all my travel issues, four days of being away from the madness of my life, and exhausting job, working with numbers is exhausting, Zoie. I hope I am not sounding so childish.'

I smile and say, 'No, Saim, you sound excited.'

I haven't heard him sound so optimistic in years. Deep down, I am so glad he is stepping out.

'Also, I have decided to put an end to my bachelorhood, you must find me a nice girl, but I would like to meet her first and get to know her before I jump into eternal bliss.' He says it with boyish enthusiasm.

'You and my mom have been after my life, so I have given both of you the responsibility to find me love, and oh please, a word of caution, my mom says the girl has to be from our community, so that narrows your search, so good luck finding someone for me, Zoie.'

I have offered my matchmaking services to Saim in the past, which he had refused, but today he sounds happy from his usual 'depressed' self. I am really delighted to hear him say all these things.

'Okay, Zoie. I have to get back to work, I will call you once I am back from my brief vacation, and who knows if all goes well I might join you at the reunion upon my return. But before you get too excited, I am not making any promises, I said I might.'

'Okay okay. Have a safe trip who knows you will find a wonderful girl in your flight and you both fall in love and marry in Dubai.'

'Seriously Zoie!!! A two-hour flight is rather short to fall in love and marry someone, plus it's Dubai, not Vegas, so please enough with the filmi romance.'

'Oh, you are so boring.' I reply.

'Yeah I know, and you are foolishly romantic. Okay, got to go stay well.'

'Godspeed Saim, don't forget to send me pictures. Bye.'

I put the phone down, thinking it's so wise that he has moved on; a change of environment would be so good for his depression. I have always wanted to talk to Saim about his depression, but could never find the courage to do so. In our culture, people don't talk about such things. It's still a taboo; which cannot be discussed openly. People don't want to associate with someone suffering from depression. Families of such individuals are ashamed to openly get help. In most cases, depression goes untreated; it's only in a few very rare cases that such individuals seek professional help, that too secretly, and the charges for therapy are insanely high. No support-groups are available to help individuals suffering from depression, due to lack of acceptability in society.

Sardonically, people make crude jokes about the dreaded *'pagal khana'*. Mental health is not something to joke about. Sadly, people don't consider it an actual disorder or a big issue. It's a common misconception that depression is merely a result of being overly sad. Often the advice given by people is to repent to the Almighty and be grateful for your blessings, but people also forget that it is a *Sunnah* to seek help for illness; be it of the mind or the body. Like any other illness, a professional should treat it.

Ironically, if a person has depression, he or she will be stigmatized even after being treated; hence it's always kept a secret. As a society, we really need to grow and acknowledge depression as an illness just like any other illness that negatively affects how you feel, the way you think or act. Fortunately, depression is treatable. Researches tell us that there are many factors that contribute to the onset of depression, this includes genetics, change in chemical or hormone level in the body, certain medical conditions or general stress, grief in life, all these, and many more can lead to depression. It could happen to anyone. Proper treatment by a medical professional is the key to recovery for the illness of the mind. Plus, friends and family of such patients should also extend a helping hand towards them. Let them know we are there for them. Maybe once Saim comes back from his vacation, I can talk to him about it, offer my help, or tell him I understand. Maybe…. I need to muster up some courage to speak to Siam.

-How is the diet going?

- Not good. I had eggs for

  breakfast.

- Scrambled?

- No! Cadbury.

The 'F' words

October.... hot & humid.

Like always, weeks quickly pass by. Aambi *Appa* landed in K-town over the weekend with just two months left for the wedding; she needs to do a few preparations for Jibbo's big day.

The three of us go on a shopping spree, and while shopping, we also took breaks to try many crazy roadside junk foods available in Karachi. I consider them my cheat-meals. My initial excitement to eat salad and drink only lemon water is tempered a little and I want to ditch my diet plan sometimes. Dreadfully, Aambi *Appa* gets sick with an upset stomach and was given intravenous electrolytes to stabilize the salts in her body, to prevent her from dehydration. *Amma*, on the other hand, has given me and Anu hell for feeding her all the junk food, which causes her to fall sick.

Amma always overreacts for no reason. I mean seriously, Anu and I ate the same stuff, but nothing happened to us. Maybe our digestive system is immune to all the bacteria and contaminations present in the food. This is the blessing of living in a densely polluted metropolis; your immune system becomes rock solid. According to the investigative shows on our local TV channels, we have rat meat in *samosa*s and only God knows what else in our food. Despite knowing all this, we Karachites are such foodies. From the new trending cafes to the shabbiest *dhaba*s, the food-lovers will travel miles and miles on pitch-dark highways to enjoy freshly made *Koyla Karahi*. Every other day something new is advertised on social media, and we blindly lineup outside those food joints to satisfy our tantalizing taste buds. This is our ultimate passion as Karachites to try new food joints.

HAPPINESS IS... How can one lose weight living in a city that offers some of the best cuisines?

eating Pani Puri

F-O-O-D is one important **F word** for us. They lade our desi dishes with oil and spices accompanied by carbs like *roti* and *rice* that make up our staple diet. So much so that the fruit we eat has sugar and *chaat masala* sprinkled generously on it. This busy city also has a sweet tooth; from piping hot *jalebie*s to the yummiest *mithaie*s to super moist cakes and cookies; we have it all. We make desserts out of vegetables, like carrots and bottle gourd. We carry huge cauldron to picnics and stuff our mouths with *Biryani*. Our weddings, festivals, even our deaths are incomplete without food. We can't imagine meeting each other without making plans for lunch or dinner, so food is a common social link between those who inhabit this city.

♣

Today I am invited to one such social meet up. It's called a committee or kitty, by whom or why? I have no clue. The mechanism of a monthly committee is that a bunch of women allocate a certain amount of money as means of saving. They give this amount each month to a person in charge of the committee, via balloting the in-charge takes out the name of one member of the committee, and they give the whole collected amount to that member. This rather complex economic system, to rotate the money, is usually followed by a get-together either at home or at a popular café for the affluent class.

There are certain codes of conduct to these get-togethers. First, an outfit is never repeated by the women in such gatherings. Second, it's okay to be fashionably late for the meetup, so everyone thinks you are super busy. The concept of Rsvp is alien for the *desi* girls. Often Rsvp is done after the party is over, to explain why one could not attend. Husband traveling to Europe on business and kids' tuition are among the most common excuses. Those who do attend are dressed to perfection with not even a hair out of place.

Keeping all the above information in my mind, I carefully choose the best outfit that I have in my wardrobe, considering its 35° degree outside, I cannot help but chose a lawn kurta to keep me cool. Finding accessories to match is another tough task. I carefully make a mental note to change my bag as I have carried the same bag in two previous meet-ups, almost committing a fashion crime. Today's get-together is a breakfast meet up, for which I have drunk only a liter of hot lemon water since morning. I can hear my stomach grouching and the echoes of my hunger-pangs reach my ears, making a sound of a broken trumpet. Suddenly, I get distracted by the loud sounds of the television. Sughra has switched on the TV to watch her favorite Morning show. The host of the show in her uncouth manner and loud voice is giving tips on weight loss and fairness. Her voice is so shrill that it hurts my ears in the room across the hall where the TV is placed. I call out Sughra and ask her to keep it low; but fail to get a reply from her. I walk towards the hall and see her awestruck by the fairness mask that is being made on the show. Finally, with the low volume and some peace in the environment, I can focus on my dressing.

After 40 minutes of meticulous dressing, I reach the venue to find the host sitting alone. OMG!! "*Am I the only one here?*" I reacted inwardly. I quickly check the WhatsApp messages to see if others are coming. The chat has 50% confirmation. I, on purpose, took a lot of time to get dressed, yet I am the first one to reach. Having no other choice, I sit by the host to give her company. A few greetings and compliments are exchanged, followed by some small-talk.

It takes a long wait and many messages by the host on the WhatsApp group for people to pour in. Time management is the nemesis of the ladies of this city, approximately one hour has passed by, from the time given on the invite, for everyone to arrive at the café and settle down. The menu is handed out and finally, foods and drinks are ordered. By now my stomach is making loud noises of a Conga being played in the jungles of Africa. I order a chicken club sandwich (in multigrain bread) with fries and a caramel Frappuccino (I am allowed some cheat-meals before the reunion and I have been waiting for so long that my stomach surely needs some compensation). Most of the ladies order eggs or salads with bulletproof coffee.

The topic of discussion was the other **F word** called **F-A-T**.

Women share their fitness regimes, the boot camps and Pilate classes they have joined, and how much effort they put in to get in their current shape. The entire committee is like a focus group on diet and beauty. A dichotomy; why have a get-together at a place that offers scrumptious food and then only talk about calories? A few ladies hardly touch the food they ordered. What a waste of money and resources, I contemplate. A few women with larger appropriations joke about cellulite deposits and big appetites as a defense-mechanism to avoid any body-shaming jokes, disguised as fitness advice. As the discussion among the ladies grows intense, I notice that it is strange to see how, as women, we are unhappy with what we have. The thinnest girl in this group is unhappy about her skin or hair. The most beautiful girl by all standards, named Salma, is unhappy because of love and relationship issues. It's funny that most of my life I equated beauty with happiness; pretty **+** thin = most happy. This was the perfect equation for a happy life; surprisingly as I meet more people, I realize there is something wrong in the above equation.

♣

Around a decade back, our city was hit by a wave of fitness and healthy eating, mostly adopted from the west. This was a welcoming addition to improve our lifestyle and was appreciated by many.

In recent years, the wave has turned into a tsunami and we have all become fixated with our weights, so much that the fixation is no longer about being happy or healthy, but it's about having a perfectly sculpted body so we can compete with others, more so for women than men. Nowadays everyone is posting *before* and *after* pictures of themselves along with pictures of their 'healthy meals' on social media; remember *you aren't healthy until you post it.* Weight loss is not only a regime for better health, but has become a multimillion-dollar industry that feeds on our insecurities as people.

It is good to be healthy and fit; *obesity* can lead to many diseases, but a few extra pounds should be forgiven. We all are not born with the same body type, genes, or metabolism. A lifestyle change should not only be in terms of weight loss, but should be more to improve our quality of life. Being happy and self-contented should also be of supreme importance. This image of a perfect body of a woman is flashed so much in front of us that it is embedded in our subconscious; anything that does not fit that image is rejected by us, collectively. We have become obsessed with our bodies. The unrealistic standards of beauty have absolutely exhausted us. We all want a photoshopped body and face that we often see on the billboards.

By the time breakfast ends, it's already time for lunch and picking up kids from school. Later in the day, I have to take *Amma* to

Tehmina Auntie's house for hi-tea. All the ladies of the families, along with their daughters, are invited, and its mandatory attendance for me and Anu, or else *Amma* will be very upset.

How can one lose weight in this city with two invitations in one day? Okay, I will skip lunch and only eat at hi-tea, and won't have dinner. With the reunion so near, I seriously need to focus on my eating, I remind myself again.

You are imperfect, permanently flawed, and you are beautiful.

-Amy Bloom

Excess Baggage

Same day in the evening

At 5:00 pm sharp, I pick my darling mom to take her to Tehmina aunty's house; she is mom's first cousin, her best friend since childhood, and huge emotional support to *Amma* after my father passed away. Tehmina aunty has one daughter, Saba, and two sons, Karim and Rahim; both sons are happily married with children. Saba is still single. I had not met Saba since Pinky made a nasty comment about her size in our last family rendezvous.

Like always, Tehmina aunty's house is full of people. She throws amazing parties; the food is always home-cooked and super tasty. As children, my sisters and I would always be eager to go to her house because of the delicious food, and that later she always gave us separate boxes to take home the yummy goodies.

Tehmina aunty sees *Amma* and me entering the house and rushes towards us to meet us.

'*Haye, kab sey intizaar kar rahi thi* (I had been waiting for so long).'

I lean towards her to give her a hug and she tightly hugs me back saying, '*Meri moti* Zoie *kaisi hai?*' Instant flashback of my childhood memories comes to haunt me; despite being so loving and caring, Tehmina aunty has a sharp tongue. My earliest memory of her is referring to me and a few other girls in the family, as *moti*, *kaali*, and *choti*, all under the pretext of love and affection. It was an expression of love but what she didn't realize and neither did many of us, young children, that she is body-shaming us.

After mingling around and meeting the other guests in the family, I go inside the kitchen to ask Saba if she needed any help. There stands Tehmina aunty by the stove, along with *Amma* and Saba. Upon seeing me enter *Amma* calls me, 'Zoie, *jaldi idhar aao.*' Thinking she needs my kitchen expertise, I rush towards her, but little did I know that it is the same nonsense all over again.

'Zoie, Saba *key liye koi rishta dhoondo,*' says Tehmina aunty in a serious yet woeful tone.

'Mein tou raat bhar sau nahi sakti, koi bhi ho, widower, divorcee *bas bachay nahi honay chahiyen. Tum* Ashoo *ki* family *mein dekho na.'*

Huh?! In a state of disbelief, I immediately turn towards Saba who is looking at the floor, blood flushed out of her face because of embarrassment.

Amma adds insult to injury by saying, 'Zoie, Saba *ko koi achi dieting bhi batao na, wohi jo tum ney ki thi shaadi sey pehley, yaad hai?'*

'*Haan haan kitni patli hogai thee* Zoie *shaadi key* time.' Tehmina aunty adds her two cents to this rather bizarre conversation.

'Stop it *Amma*, just stop you two,' I reply angrily, 'You know she is trying very hard, so enough of this trashing-your-own-daughter conversation. Saba is beautiful and highly educated. A man will be lucky to have her in his life.'

'*Haan haan*, her face is pretty but *thora* weight *kum karleti tou* proposals *aatey na, Abb* age *bhie horahi hai iski*,' adds Tehmina aunty.

'No, aunty, you need to stop. All my life you have called me fat, someone else dark, and now your own daughter? Do you realize that you are hurting us all deep down, making us feel unworthy? You both, as our mothers, should give us confidence, rather than body-shaming us because you fear the world more than you love your own children. And you *Amma*, you have always called me fat when I was four, when I was 24, and now that I am forty, I am still fat for you. This family seriously needs to grow up and stop hurting its precious girls. And enough with this '*shaadi nahi hogi*' crap, *nahi hogi koi baat nahi* life will not end, there are other fulfilling things in life for her to do.'

I grab Saba's hand and drag her out of that hostile kitchen. I can hear *Amma* and Tehmina aunty murmur in the background, *'Isko kitna ghussa aata hai, koi baat karo bas naraaz ho jati hai.'*

After years, I feel this light. The excess baggage I was carrying for years is finally off my back. People around us are that way; every time they see a person who is struggling with weight, they will only comment on that person's weight gain or loss, as if that's the only intelligent conversation they can do.

 For the rest of the evening, I stayed away from *Amma* and her cousin. Later *Amma* and I drove back in complete silence till I dropped her home.

♣

We all live in a fairly conservative society, especially when it comes to women. Being married and living in a secure home with children and a husband is the perfect picture drawn for our gender, yet many women are still single because they are *unmarriageable*. Why should any woman be called "unmarriageable"? One of the most common reason is body image. Our men are told that they will only win the most beautiful girl as a trophy wife. Any girl who **does not** fit the profile of a fair, thin girl, having longhair with a beautiful face, most importantly who has perfect cooking skills and will live with *Ammi Jee,* is not *marriage-material.* She needs to be educated enough to have manners but not an opinion. The age, just like an expiration date, also plays an important role in the above scenario. The purpose of marriage is to find peace, love and companionship; sadly, we have made it all about looks and outer beauty.

I sit in my car, thinking how badly women are objectified by their own gender. How our worth is mostly in our bodily image. A woman's most appreciated skills are that in the kitchen which to an extent is appreciated, but it should not be her only achievement.

Her other accomplishments should not take a back-seat.

Consumed by my thoughts, I take a deep breath and look outside the window of my car. Everyone seems to be in a hurry, like they are getting late to reach somewhere. At that moment, my phone makes a tinkling sound, I look at the screen, and it's a WhatsApp from Dina. I open the picture she sent.

I couldn't help but laugh.

WAQT KAM

Mid–October….. finally some rain.

Three days of pouring and the city is already flooded. Open main holes, sewage water oozing from every corner, 72 hours without electricity, and garbage floating on the streets. Despite all the above, the trees look greener, 'Petrichor' lingers in the air……

Almost 2 weeks left for the reunion, and the lemon water is giving me bouts of acidity. I don't even want to look at anything green. I am human, not a goat who should be happily eating leaves. I so want to cheat, hot *roghni naan,* and some *butter chicken*; these are the sinister thoughts in my mind. The damn weighing scale is not helping either. Maybe I am having inch loss, but I decide not to check due to the fear of unfavorable results.

To distract my mind from the harsh possibilities of not losing an inch, I check my phone and read the latest news about the national and international state of affairs.

"*Mahwish Hayat **Slut-shamed** once again for receiving Tamgha-e-Imtiaz*", is one of the many headlines. Another one: "*Mahwish Hayat gives a befitting reply to all the haters in her recent interview*". Sadly, the internet trolls have lost all senses of decency. So many months have passed by since she was adorned with the prestigious award, yet those who disapprove are still brutal in their odious comments. What kind of intolerable society do we live in? Why can't we disagree amicably? Why do we have to character assassin a woman to prove our point? I thought body-shaming was enough, but slut-shaming is way out of line. To disagree with the decision of Hayat's nomination is one thing, but to say she slept her way up the ladder is way awry, and no, it's not allowed because she is an actress. Desolately, it's a professional hazard that our actresses face being in the entertainment industry. Many women in our culture also endure such shaming, especially if they have a broken relationship or they dare to move on in life. The licentious comments about a woman's character show the decaying fiber of our society. What kind of mindset does our society have to say something so revolting and derogatory about another human being?

Scrolling down, another interesting news in Huff Post catches my attention, ***"Fabulously FAT rat rescued after getting stuck in manhole cover"***, followed by a picture of a rat stuck between the tiny holes of a manhole cover. This is probably the only time **Fabulous** is used before **FAT** in leading news.

The third news that amazes me is about a plus-size woman who climbed Kilimanjaro, Africa's highest mountain. How impressive.

Maybe I should try climbing an actual mountain, but the thought of mountain-climbers in my HIIT class is enough to convince me otherwise.

What kind of crazy world is this? I wonder, reading the news.

Getting absolutely bored, I decide to message Saim to ask him about his trip, and to inquire if he tried all the delectable food places I had texted him. I also want to give my feedback on the business idea he had discussed, but most important of all, I want to ask him if he is coming to the reunion or not. As I pick my phone up, it rings, showing a call from my mom. By the time I am done talking with *Amma*, I have no energy to call Saim.

Eternal Peace

End of October

At 7:00 in the evening, Muhammad throws a tantrum for no reason. He refuses to eat what is cooked at home, stubbornly demands that I order a Happy Meal for him. Being a helicopter mom and trying to follow a healthy regime, I tell him that junk food during the week is a complete no. He makes the saddest face and tells me he will stay hungry. I look him in the eye and tell him "suit yourself".

After 15 minutes of being strong and ignoring Muhammad, thinking he will eat what's available, **"*mom guilt*"** crawls inside my heart. *Mom guilt* is the feeling of guilt experienced by moms who think they suck at motherhood. The thought of Muhammad, my baby, sleeping hungry for the entire night is enough to shake the health freak out of me. I try to convince him that on weekend we will get a Happy Meal, but my God, this kid is so stubborn, reminds me of his *phupo*. He has surely not taken anything from my side of the gene-pool. Finally, after much bargaining, we settle for instant noodles - albeit not the healthiest meal - but at least it is somewhat home-cooked.

As I stand near the stove waiting for the water to boil, my phone rings.

The screen on my Samsung Galaxy flashes the name "Irfan Nizami". I take about two seconds to juggle around with my memory and realize who Irfan Nizami is. Irfan was a batch-mate in college. We took a few courses together, but he used to hang out with Saim a lot. Never knew I had his number saved in my phone. Why is he calling me, I wonder.

I pick up the phone and without sounding too surprised, I say 'Hello' with a straight voice.

'Assalam-o-Alaikum Zoya, this is Irfan. I have some bad news for you. You were in touch with Saim, right?'

'Ah yes, I am.' I reply, feeling clueless.

'Zoya, sadly, Saim passed away today in the afternoon, he went to work and after lunch, his colleagues saw that he kept his head on the table. When he didn't move for an hour, everyone thought he must have dozed off, a colleague from work went to wake him up. The minute he touched him, Saim fell on the floor. They called the ambulance, but he was long gone before he could reach the hospital. It was sudden cardiac arrest.'

Staggered, I feel my knees locked, my body roots to the ground and my mind numb from the noise in my surroundings. I can slowly feel my heart sinking and a sense of disbelief overcomes all my senses. I don't remember for how long I stayed in this position, looking blankly at my phone, trying to make some sense of what I just heard.

The next morning after *Fajar* prayers, I sit in the balcony to look at the sky. I didn't get much sleep the previous night, a part of me was still in disbelief and another part of me was fed up with the innumerable messages regarding Saim's demise that flooded my inbox. Irfan was kind enough to update me regarding the address and timings of Saim's funeral prayers. Ashoo was very supportive and gave me space by putting the kids to bed and keeping it quiet.

Around 12:30 in the afternoon, I follow the directions sent by Irfan and reach Saim's house. Men dressed in *kurta shalwar* have crowded the gate. A small section of the garden is segregated for women; I enter the female section and see a few familiar faces. A lady in white is telling everyone that the mother of the deceased is inside the house as many people are looking for her. I did not have the courage to meet her so I sat on the corner of the white sheet spread on the ground, words of Funeral *Dua* on my mind and a certain fear and disbelief in my heart. A crying sound from a distance brings me back to reality. Soft whispers of the *Kalimah* being recited (*There is no God but Allah, and Muhammad (peace be upon him) is His messenger*) fills the air. I immediately get up and move towards the entrance of the segregated area, a few women are already standing there looking towards the other section.

Shaken to my core, I look outside and see a white-shrouded body covered with a sheet being carried on a metal bed like coffin. The irregular murmur of the *Kalimah* slowly gives way to loud recitations that echo in the air. Men line up to pay their final respects to the deceased by carrying the mortal remains one by one. Uncontrollable tears trickle down from my eyes and a lump sticks in my throat, I can hear my heartbeat and the only words that echo in my mind are: *"O Allah! Forgive him and have mercy upon him"*.

After sitting in the corner for a while, a bit disoriented from my surroundings, I grasp that grief is something we swallow slowly, drop by drop until we find complete closure, and forget about the reality of leaving this world someday never to return. We bury our thoughts quicker than the body of our dear ones. I get up to leave Saim's house. Upon reaching the gate, I see Irfan standing with a group of people. Most of the men have attended the funeral prayers at the *masjid* and came back to Saim's home. Nowadays very few close people accompany the immediate family to the graveyard for the final rituals of burial. Upon seeing me look for my car, Irfan calls out my name. I move towards the group of people standing with Irfan; they are all familiar faces from college, but the names are all mixed up at this moment. I stand quietly next to Irfan. All of us look disturbed as Saim was our age; we all stand there silently trying to absorb the reality called *death*.

Funerals are surely for the living; the dear departed is handling the matters of the soul whereas the rituals related to the body are for those still alive, to make them realize that the same body which they so preciously own will soon be under piles of soil.

After a deafening silence of few minutes, one person in the group says how shocked he is to hear about the *untimely* death of Saim, another person says that depression got the best of him, the third one comment that depression and isolation are silent killers. I look at all of them, absolutely stunned. I turn towards Irfan and ask him, 'Did everyone know he was suffering from depression?'

'Yes Zoya, everyone knew he was going through a tough time; he had isolated himself from everyone because he had gotten very big in size and didn't feel like meeting people.' He replies.

A sudden sense of resentment and despair fills my mind and I ask, Irfan and everyone around, a question, but deep down I know I am asking myself:

'If we all knew he was going through a tough time, why didn't we extend our help when he was alive?' I say sounding angry.

My question is followed by pin-drop silence and then after a few seconds Irfan replies:

'I don't know, Zoya, we thought he needed space, people don't like to talk about depression let alone accept help.' I stare at him muted and then with culpability and heaviness in my heart, I quietly leave the group and move towards my car to reach home.

That night, lying in bed, I kept on thinking about death, in general, and Saim, in particular, how miserable and lonely he had been for so many years. How we, as his so-called friends, never reached out to him for help. How we never stood up with him to lessen his pain. Maybe, only maybe, if a few of us had taken the time and effort from our busy lives to help this friend in need. Sadly, for many years, Saim lived an unhappy life. Just when he was trying his best to find some solace and a bit of relief, his time was up.

"Mortal remains - that's what we all become in the end; beauty, looks, talent, and slowly even memories perish into nothingness. To Allah we belong and towards HIM shall we return."

And it took cutting back the prettiest parts of myself to finally realize that this shell does not define me.

For I am so much more than the flesh and bones that case the beautiful tragedies of my heart and mind.

- Becca Lee

Paradigm Shift

Beginning of November

3:30 pm. I leave the house to pick Dina; she had gone to Islamabad for some personal commitment and could not attend Saim's funeral. Today we are going to our weekly Qur'an class. Many years ago, Dina and I connected ourselves to divine teachings to find some inner peace. It was probably one of the best decisions of our lives, but sadly every week something would come up and we would miss most of our classes. Recently, we both have been feeling very down and reconnected with the miraculous scripture of the Almighty.

We both sit quietly in the car, both scared and disturbed by Saim's death. He was our age, and went to meet his Creator. This is how short and unpredictable life is. Our daily routine consumes our days and months that we never stop for a minute to understand and ponder upon the real purpose of our temporary lives. Why are we sent to this world? And what legacy we hope to leave behind should be among our worries. Sadly, the reality is otherwise; most of us never think about our ultimate destination, we feel we are indispensable. These weekly classes are at least a way to find some serenity and focus in our busy and day-to-day lives.

Upon reaching the venue, we quickly settle inside the class, in front of us is our beautiful and blessed Qur'an teacher sitting behind a table, a laptop, and a mic placed in front of her. The huge projector on the wall displays a beautiful *Dua* about the purity of our intentions and asking Allah for guidance.

She starts the lecture with her usual *Dua* and salutation to the Prophet Muhammad (PBUH) before she unveils the hidden treasures in the Divine revelation.

'Today we will talk about **YOU**.' She says in a casual voice.

A bit surprised, many in the audience, including me, look around.

'Why are you all looking surprised?' she adds, 'It's a fact that deep down we all want to only talk and hear things about ourselves, right?

Well! Guess what the Qur'an talks about you' – **"The Perfect YOU"**.

Feeling a bit intrigued, I quickly put my phone on silent mode and slide it in my bag so I can focus without being distracted.

The teacher begins her talk: 'In many verses, Allah Almighty has clearly described the creation of Human being as the *perfectly created.*'

"We have indeed created humankind in the best of molds." [1]

And in another verse Allah says:

"Then We made the sperm into a clot of congealed blood; then of that clot, We made a (fetus) lump; then we made out of that lump bones and clothed the bones with flesh; then we developed out of it another creature. So blessed be Allah, the best to create!"[2]

And also, in *Surah Namal*, the Qur'an says:

---

[1](Quran 95:4) (Surat At-Tin, The Fig)
[2](Quran 23:14) (Surat Al-Mu'minun, The Believers)

"The work of Allah who has perfected everything (He created)."[3]

'Whatever the Almighty has created, HE has created to perfection; look at the entire Universe around you. The Creator then placed humans on top of everything. These verses not only speak of the human beings' physical form but also speak of the perfection and purity of the human spirit and the human Will. It broadens our horizon and makes us realize the various dimensions of our existence, our emotional competence, inquisitiveness, our desire to excel, our powerful ability to love without bounds; and our yearning for Allah, even when we do not acknowledge it.'

'See, how clearly Allah, the Almighty, is speaking about you. The Creator is addressing you with so much love and a lot of pride in creating you to perfection.'

She pauses and looks right at me as if talking to me.

---

[3](Quran 27:88) (Surah Al-NAMAL, The Ants)

'Do we realize how often we are critical of ourselves; we find faults in our faces and bodies, sometimes many faults. We criticize our features; our nose, our eyes, our skin color. We have issues of insecurity surrounding our body and appearance; I think all of us do.'

She continues: The Omnipotent is addressing 'You', by saying:

"He is the One Who has made perfectly everything He has created: He began the creation of human beings with clay, And made his progeny from a quintessence of the nature of a fluid despised: But He fashioned him in due proportion, and breathed into him something of His spirit."[4]

'Do you realize how immensely profound it is when Allah says that He *breathed into us* something of His spirit!; Me, You, your children, your families, the poor beggar on the road, the physically challenged even the

---

[4](Quran 32:7-9) (As-Sajdah, the Prostration)

disbelievers, all are HIS creations and created perfect in every way because HE created us.'

'So what does that mean for me and you to see ourselves as perfect?' She pauses, allowing the question to sink in.

'I want all of you to take a moment and ask yourself this question, without falling into self-pity or viewing yourself as flawed,' a pause by her again and complete silence in the surrounding. 'Take out a mirror from your purse, if you don't have one, take out your phones and switch on the camera, put it on selfie mode and look at yourself.'

Unsure if she is serious or just joking, most of us hesitate and look at each other.

'Come on, I am serious. Please switch on your selfie modes, and please don't start clicking pictures or checking the inbox for messages,' she says in a joyful tone, the room is once again filled with laughter.

'Tell me, what it means to look at ourselves and see a perfect creation of Allah. No matter how different our features are from each other, do we not feel immense gratitude towards the Almighty?'

I sit there, looking at myself in my phone. I feel good about myself. The same phone that I have used many times to click my pictures and hating them later. I close my phone and place it back in my bag.

The teacher continues, 'How can we find faults in what Allah has created? How can we criticize what Allah has blessed us with? A believer is always grateful.'

'Feel grateful, and with gratitude in your heart protect your body, eat healthy, stay away from diseases by taking care of yourself, because a healthy body will lead to a healthy mind, and a healthy mind will then think about its capacity to reach the various heights of *Imaan* (faith).' We all nod in agreement, this is something we all knew but today it seems we are hearing it for the first time.

'Ignite in yourself an intellectual rigor and strive to be extraordinary, like the best people of the religion, they were only extraordinary people because they accepted HIS words and were thankful to Allah for HIS many Blessings. Don't limit your body to basic desires and pseudo-body images. Think of what your mind and heart can achieve,'

'Easier said than done, right?' She takes a sip of water from the crystal glass placed on the corner of the table next to her laptop.

'We will soon go back to our respective lives, in this perfection-driven world. The unlimited desires of our '*nafs*' like an insatiable monster will surround us. Human beings are over-pressurized by the society around us, to look a certain way, our skin color, weight, features, height even our age is put under a microscope more often than we would like, reminding me of Hitler.' She says blatantly.

'Let me share a story with you today, whenever you feel unsure about your worth, think of this story. It is a story of the lesser-known Companion of Prophet Muhammad (peace and blessings be upon him). His name was '*Julaybib*' which means *"small grown"*. The name indicates that Julaybib was small and short, like a dwarf. More than that, he is described as being "damim" which means ugly, deformed, or of repulsive appearance.

Julaybib's lineage (family line) was not known, the society in which he lived took pride in lineage, and there was no record of his parents. All that we know of him was that he was an Arab, and he was one of the Ansar, and he wasn't handsome, in fact, he was short, ugly, and on top of that, he was disabled. The disabilities under which Julaybib lived would have been enough to have him ridiculed and shunned in any society, but he, as a human, needed love and companionship just like anyone else. The Prophet of Mercy (peace be upon him) was also aware of the needs and sensibilities of his humble companion. With Julaybib in mind, the Prophet (PBUH) went to one of the *Ansar* and asked his daughter's hand in marriage for Julaybib. It is said that the daughter of the *Ansari* man was known for her beauty and that there was none among the women of that clan who could compete with her looks. The *Ansari* man and his wife, upon hearing the proposal of Julaybib, were not in favor of this marriage, but when the daughter found out, she asked her parents to accept it on her behalf and not refuse the Prophet of Allah. Upon hearing her answer, the Prophet (PBUH) made *dua*s for her, she was then married to the most disliked and body-shamed man in society. It is said that they both were together till Julaybib was bestowed with Martyrdom. The Prophet said for Julaybib: *"O' Allah he is from me and I am from him"[5]*, surely an honor for anyone if the Prophet (PBUH) would say such words.'

'This story has many lessons for us, some obvious, some not so obvious, giving us room to ponder upon the many aspects of our short lives in this world and the things we give priority, but the most important lesson is that the man who was shunned and body-shamed by many had a special place in the eyes of the Almighty. Now please, this does not mean that every time we are body-shamed, at a get-together or a party, we should think of our higher level, let's not get carried away.' Laughter again fills the surroundings.

'All I am saying is that body-shaming has existed in **ignorant societies**. its pure ignorance that we measure all human beings with the same yardstick. Sadly, but honestly, we all have done it to someone without acknowledging it, but remember that it is

---

[5](Sahih-Muslim, Book 3, Hadith No. 1861)

disliked by our faith to take out faults in people. Allah says,

"O you, who have believed, let not a people ridicule [another] people; perhaps they may be better than them, nor let women ridicule [other] women; perhaps they may be better than them. And do not insult one another and do not call each other by [offensive] nicknames. Wretched is the name of disobedience after [one's] faith. And whoever does not repent - then it is those who are the wrongdoers."[6]

'What happens when you continuously call a person with an offensive nickname or point out his or her flaws, that person will fall in self-doubt, will build a negative self-concept about himself, that person will also start detesting you, may even gossip about you or have bad sentiments for you. All this will not only spoil the person's own self-esteem but also your relationship with him.'

'Lastly, let me sum up everything for you all, Allah has made you perfect the way you are, your skin color, your features all are given by HIM; feel His blessings and live with this liberty of being the perfect creation. Embrace

---

[6](Quran 49:11) (Al-Hujuraat - The Chambers)

this freedom to accept yourself, and take care of your physical and mental health, love yourself, and allow yourself to love others for the sake of Allah, and focus on living a worthy and meaningful life.'

She ends her lecture with a beautiful *Dua* making many of us feel worthy and important.

Dina and I leave the class quietly. As I wait outside for my car, I feel the sun beaming right at me, the humidity in the air making every inch of my body sticky, and the wind blowing directly on my face; I take a deep breath and realize that I, like many other people in this world, was searching for acceptance in the wrong places, *when it was always in front of me, in the Book of GOD, telling me how special I am. If only I could rise above from my petty self and appreciate my worth.*

Being a M-A-N

Mid-November.... *Karachi ki thandi sham*

6:00 pm. Dina is honking outside my gate. Before rushing down, I give last-minute instructions to Ashoo about food on the stove, 'Ashoo, please eat on time. I have made separate burgers for the kids, they are in the kitchen, please eat home-cooked food, no ordering from outside.' I request him, which sounds more like an order.

'Zo, we know, please go and enjoy yourself, you are only going for a few hours, not for a month.' Ashoo says looking through his reading-glasses that he puts so precisely at the center of his nose, giving a seductive look.

I call Hamza's name twice, but he was busy playing PS4, with large headphones placed on his ears, absolutely oblivious of his surroundings. As I am about to walk towards him to give him a few instructions, Ashoo immediately gets up from his seat and hugs me, dragging me towards the door. He hands me my black and red clutch and says bye for the third time.

'Zo, please go, Dina is honking. She's been waiting. Have a good time and don't worry we all will behave ourselves as per your instructions.' He says in a cynical tone.

Looking at the clock near the door, I hurry down, hopping the stairs. Dina is waiting for me by the gate in her wine-color Toyota Fortuner. Pervaiz graciously opens the door for me; I quickly get inside to see a beautifully dressed Dina in black chiffon shirt, eyes meticulously painted with a silver-blue shimmery eye-shadow, and a thin liner to give her brown eyes definition.

'Hello, sorry, I came down late, giving last-minute instructions.' I quickly say in my defense.

'No problem Zoie. Oh! My my! I Love your shirt. Wow! You look so pretty.' She compliments me with a big smile.

'Dina, you look smashing, too. We are both wearing black just like old college days when we used to get dressed; it will be so much fun.' I reply with enthusiasm.

With mutual admiration in our eyes and a lot of excitement, we were off to the annual reunion.

As we enter the gate of our Alma Mater, we are greeted by the gate-keeper *Baba* Ghafoor. He has gone so old since I last recall him. The walls of the campus are freshly painted, and the courtyard is decorated with red and black net with "Welcome Alumni" written on the sides. For a moment, it seems like another life when Dina and I would roam between the corridors of these walls, full of ambition to change the world.

The stage is decorated with the college logo, a shield with wings in red and navy blue. A young girl in her twenties is on stage, holding the microphone announcing, ' *This event is once again set to be an exciting opportunity to return to your place of study and meet up with old friends; an evening of reminiscing and reconnection. We will start the event shortly. In the meantime, you all are* requested to have a look around the campus and enjoy the welcome drinks.'

Dina and I walk past the entrance hall; I am surprised to see a sea of people in front of us. Some familiar faces, some unknown faces, among the crowd that fills the space ahead of us. The right side of the main event area has pictures of higher achievers from the alumni, who have made the College proud. The left wall is full of pictures of people who are no longer in this world; pictures of a few dear teachers, some staff members hang on the walls with a brief memorial obituary written beneath each photograph. Suddenly, among the collage of photos, my eyes spot a picture of a beautiful young boy with a bright smile. It's an old picture of Saim, from our college days, his eyes full of life and his smile full of braces. Written underneath his framed photo, **'Lives are like rivers, eventually, they go where they must, not where we want them to'.**

I stand in front of his picture for a moment and thought, Saim will always be a part of all our reunions from now. He may not be here in person, but he surely is in spirit.

The rest of the evening is a mix of memories, some good and some not so good. Irfan spots me in the crowd and comes over to say hello. He reintroduced me to a few people whom I had completely forgotten about. We share some old jokes, some memories rejoiced. Zaheer, the biggest prankster of our days in college, joins the rest of us; he has not changed a bit, still makes loud and repulsive jokes.

In the hustle of the evening, one name is mentioned many times, that one person is the center of everyone's joke. A boy called Tahir, who was in our class but was often made fun of because of his *effeminate gestures* and *shrill voice*. He was often called Tahir-a in class by many of us and we all laughed at how he moves his hands while talking. Zaheer would imitate his walk in the cafeteria and we all would laugh at it.

Flashbacks of our college days, as Zaheer imitates Tahir again; he also makes a nasty comment about Tahir's receding hair-line. Poor Tahir stands there, embarrassed as always; dreading coming to the reunion. I stand nearby witnessing all this, and somehow it was not funny anymore. It sounds rude and crude. For a minute I get surprised why in the past I laughed at something so hideous. I feel mortified for being a part of this horrendous humor. Why didn't I say something decades back to stop this from escalating? Feeling ashamed of myself, I move forward to do something.

'Stop it, Zaheer. You are being rude.' I say immediately.

'Oh, come on Zoya, it's just a joke.' He replies, feeling no guilt.

Dina is quick to join me and makes a sarcastic comment about Zaheer and his awful sense of humor.

'Zoya is right, Zaheer. You have a terrible sense of humor. It wasn't funny then, and surely it's even nastier now. And seriously, you need to grow up, whatever your insecurities are, just stop taking them out on Tahir.'

In awe, I look at Dina; she is so on fire. She gives Zaheer the forfeit reply which he deserves.

Thankfully for Zaheer, the music plays in the background and everyone's attention is towards the stage. Our Dean Mrs. Naseeruddin gives a beautiful welcome-speech to the Alumni, and the crowd cheers her every word.

Later, when dinner is served, my eyes search for Tahir. He is sitting at a table with a few people. I walk towards him and ask him if I can have a word with him. We both move towards the side.

'I am very sorry, Tahir.' I apologize.

'For what, Zoya?' he asks innocently.

"For laughing with Zaheer, when I should have taken a stand. I feel ashamed that because of the silence of many like me, you had to go through the worst humiliation during the best days of your life."

Tahir stares at me in absolute disbelief. Then after a few seconds, he responds, 'it is okay, Zoya; Zaheer has a terrible sense of humor. It was mainly him.' He says in a forgiving voice.

'I am sorry. I should have said something then, but I will tell you one thing Tahir, you are more of a man than Zaheer will ever be. It takes dignity and patience to be a man and you, my friend, are manlier than anyone else in this group. You never stoop to their level, and you acted so mature all those years, but I wish if you had punched him in the face the first time he made fun of you.'

He blushes and looks at me with amazement; and says, 'Violence is a sign of weakness, not strength.'

I nod my head in agreement.

On my way back from the reunion, I have just one thought in my mind; just like pseudo-standards of beauty for women, we have pseudo-standards of manhood, too. How easily men are ridiculed if they walk or talk in a particular manner. How, in our society, we have confused gender roles. Men would only be considered manly if they curse; smoke, love sports and are ready for a fist-fight at a drop of a hat. Young boys, who are not sporty enough, are made fun of by their peers. Teenage boys are in continuous pressure to follow the stereotypical standards of the male gender set by our society. Young adults are shammed and ridiculed for their receding hair-line, for being non-muscular, not having enough facial hair, and even for their height and voice. Is the strength of a man only in the number of muscles he has on his body? We, as a society, need to rethink our standards.

Good women do exist, but our stomachs are not flat and we talk back.

(Anonymous)

JIBBO Ki Shaadi

December.... is finally here.

One joy of life is to see the kids, who grew up in front of you, turning into mature and humble adults. Jibbo is one such kid. He was the first baby in our house and we all love him dearly. To see him planning his life with a loving partner is such a joy. Jibbran has arrived a week before the wedding, along with his father Sikander *Bhai*, his fiancée Nina and her parents.

Another delight is to see that the next generation is wiser and more sensible in spending hard-earned money. Jibbo and Nina have clearly told both the set of families that they are against ostentatious weddings that have a series of pointless events. After much convincing, the families decide to have *Nikkah* in the Mosque followed by one reception, where the guests of both bride and groom will be invited. Jibbran and Nina both have asked their parents not to get carried away and waste money on clothes and other such stuff that would not be worn or used again, they both want the guests to not give gifts (*salami*) and donate that amount to their favorite charity, to which *Amma* along with the rest of the family threw a fit.

'Why can't we have the guests give the gift amount to our favorite charity?'Asks Jibbo rather innocently.

'*Yeh larka pagal hogaya hai.*' *Amma* reacts typically.

'Jibbo *beta,* we don't ask our guest's such things in this part of the world,' Sikander *Bhai* tells him.

'We have to respect the sensibilities of our culture.' He further adds.

'I understand that it is a noble idea, but we will be giving explanations to the whole family,' comments Aambi *Apa*.

Ashoo agrees with Jibbo. Anu and I aren't sure; if our extended family is ready for such ideas, we better stay out of this discussion, but Jibbran had made up his mind and told us that he himself will donate the amount to his favorite charity. Undoubtedly, Jibbran's compassion for the less privileged is admirable; if the new generation continues to break the norms, then we really have hope for the future.

♣

Finally, the wedding day is here, it's a beautiful sunny day; Karachi's famous *'December ki dhoop'*. The cool breeze of the Arabian Sea makes the temperature drop a few notches for the people of the city. I spend the entire morning preparing for the wedding; I drink a lot of cucumber-infused water to keep my skin hydrated. By mid-day, Anu, along with Aambi *Apa,* picks me and the three of us go to the salon to get dolled up for Jibbo's big day.

We reach the venue half an hour earlier, dressed in my teal and maroon outfit with smokey eyes, giving my face a glam look. I inspect myself in the mirror placed near the entrance. Mehr has done an amazing job with the outfit; it has a beautiful silhouette and is giving my figure a slimmer look. After all, the physical hard work of so many months has paid off in the form of a healthier me. I may not have achieved the ultimate target of being the quintessential beauty, but I feel a lot more confident. Despite the confidence, a certain fear lurks in my heart as people in my circle are quick in body-shaming.

Anu arrives wearing a dazzling emerald-green and silver *Banarsi Sari* with her wedding jewels. Aambi *Apa* is dressed in an angelic white Chantal Lace outfit, looks ravishing, she is the stunning and proud mother of the groom. *Amma* walks in wearing her favorite grey color, she compliments the three of us sisters for looking so pretty, a bit shocked by her appreciation, we all giggle with joy. The men of our family are dressed in black suits. After some time, the guests start to pour in. When the venue is full of guests, Ashoo announces, '*Ladies and gentlemen, we present to you the bride and the groom.*'

A spotlight follows Jibbo and Nina as they entered the venue hand in hand. Jibbran, dressed in a Navy-blue *sherwani*, holding the hand of his bride Nina, dressed in an ivory, gold *lehenga* paired with emerald jewels. They both look so gorgeous together. Later, Dina also came with her hubby and kid, wearing a ruby red outfit.

The wedding hall is bustling with a festive aura, decorated beautifully with white flowers and dim lights; there is laughter and happiness in the air. The three of us sisters are standing together getting our pictures clicked with the groom. Anu and I step down from the stage to meet all the guests, and immediately I spot Zarina in the crowd. She walks towards me waving her hand, dressed in a fitted sky-blue sequence long shirt with gold caprice pants.

'Hello, Zoie. How are you?' She leans forward to hug me, 'Lovely décor of the venue. Zoie, the flowers look exquisite.' She adds, completely ignoring to comment about the way I look. So typical of her, I reckon.

Anu sees us talking and joins us, 'Hello, Zarina *baji*. How are you?' She asks politely.

'OMG! Is this you Anaya? I hardly recognized you; you have gained so much weight. How old is the baby?' She asks.

Embarrassed and uncomfortable, Anu replies, 'He is almost 2.'

'And you still have the pregnancy weight, I thought, you just delivered. You used to be so thin, you must do something about it Anaya or else you will never be able to lose it. Join a gym or do keto diet,' is her unsolicited advice.

I see Anu's mood being spoiled in a second, she says something in her defense and tried to give explanations, but she sounds more irritated.

For a minute, I am relieved that today it's not me whom Zarina is body-shaming, but I feel terrible for Anu. She has been putting in so much effort and yet people so easily body-sham her. I have to do something to put an end to this *Zarina Chapter*. I have some old scores to settle.

'Listen Zarina, every time you see us, you have to tell us we are fat,' I say immediately.

'We are happy with our body and we don't need your advice, we are happy and healthy, so keep your slimming advice to yourself. It is not a must for you to make everyone feel bad about their body so you can feel good about yourself. Yes, we get it, you are thin, do you need a medal for it? You think you're giving your precious advice, no you are body-shaming, which is offensive and rude.' I say all this with an ironic smile.

'Dinner is served; please enjoy the food. Oh! Sorry, we are not serving vegetable juice on the menu, now if you'll excuse us we have to see to our other guests.'

I grab Anu's hand and move towards the stage, never looked back to check the reaction on Zarina's face, but I can assume it's of utter shock.

Sometimes it is important to give a shut-up call to the regular *body-shamers*, for one's own sanity and peace of mind.

We move to the area where food is being served, Sikandar *Bhai* has selected a simple yet tasteful Desi menu. The best part about a *Desi* wedding is the yummy food and rich desserts. I wonder, would the wedding be this much fun, if we had served garden salad without dressing, kale juice, steamed vegetable, hot water and handed out Stevia sashes for dessert. Aggh! I would n-e-v-e-r want to go to such a wedding, for sure.

Later in the evening, Anu and Hamza make a small surprise presentation for Jibbo and his bride, with pictures of Jibbo's childhood, his first day in school, and many family events. Being the aunt of the groom, I was in most of the pictures, suddenly the blast from the past makes me appreciate how fresh and thin I look in these pictures, but in the year when that particular picture was taken, I never felt this way, I always despised my pictures. Why is that after decades I love the same pictures that I so hated? Why was I so unhappy with my appearance in that particular year?

I apprehend that all these years I was unhappy with my appearance because deep down *I* was body-shaming *myself*. **Body-shaming by people is nasty but body-shaming by one's own self is lethal.** Why did I waste all these years trying to get the approval of others? No matter how much thinner I got, I was never thin enough. There was always someone thinner, prettier, and smaller than my smallest size.

"And I said to my body, softly, I want to be your friend. It took a long breath and replied, "I have been waiting my whole life for this".

\- Nayyirah Waheed

Love thy Impossible

February……. This is spring for us.

'1-love, 2–love, excellent shot, 2-All' says Ashoo, as we play badminton on the roof of our small apartment building. Spring has just arrived, and the evening has a cool breeze and a pleasant vibe. Ashoo has recently bought a badminton racket set and a net. On Sunday, Hamza and Ashoo tied it to the light poles on the roof and announced that there will be a family tournament in the afternoon.

The first game is between Ashoo and me, and so far the score is 2-All. Ashoo had been a good badminton player in his college days, but with the responsibilities of being the breadwinner of the family, his passion for sports is sidelined because of his busy schedule. Today, he is playing after many years showing off his moves to the rest of us. I am a bit of an amateur. The game is getting intense, the score is 8-All, Muhammad is jumping and screaming '*come on mama, come on mama*'; Hamza is trying his best to be neutral, not to choose sides between his parents.

Finally, after running around the roof and playing to the best of my capability, Ashoo wins the match. Muhammad screams and comes running towards me giving me a hug, Ashoo screams from the other side of the net "Well played, Zo", he claps with one hand and his badminton racket in the other hand. '*Chalo* who is next, who wants to play with papa?', '*me, me*' are the sounds that fill the air.

I walk towards the side and sit on one of the few chairs placed near the entrance of the roof. While drinking water from my bottle, I appreciate how my stamina has improved, the exercise that I dread doing every morning has slowly paid off in the form of a healthier me. I am amazed how much I enjoyed this little game of badminton, an excellent form of cardio with running and jumping, yet I haven't looked at my watch once while playing with Ashoo. It is rather sad how these days our every move is counted; 30 minutes on the treadmill, 2 sets of 25 lunges, 30 squats, 10,000 steps on my Fitbit, seriously our whole day is spent counting. It is nice to break free from the mechanical aspect of the physical exercise and to just enjoy the movement of the muscle and the racing pulse. How carefree and easy it becomes when we don't have a speedometer attached.

Unarguably, the outdoor is the best place, the sky with the sun beaming from the clouds and the wind blowing through one's sweaty clothes giving a certain chill down the spine. I sit there looking at their game and thinking how much fun and relief it is to just run around without worrying about the number of calories I have burned, or that anything less than 45 minutes of physical activity will not put my body into fat-burning-mode or the worries of a pre- or post-workout meal.

I feel happy and content; feelings that have been missing for so long. The visual of Ashoo teaching the kids how to play, that we can actually enjoy physical activity as a family, is all so overwhelming. How could I have been so ungrateful all these years? The Almighty has given me the blessing of a perfectly functioning body, a healthy life, yet I showed no gratitude. In attaining the scanty standards of beauty, we women often forget to do self-love. *Self-love* doesn't mean you are selfish; it's just a revolution of mind that connects your heart to your soul. Sitting there, I make a promise to myself, to love myself from now onwards, a love that has been the most impossible thing for me for a very long time.

The sun is setting like an orange balloon, splattering its redness all over the horizon; the call of *Maghreb Adhan* fills the air. We pack our things and go down to say our prayers. After a while, Muhammad screams and jumping up and down,' I want *Faboola*, I want *Faboola*'.

'It's not *Faboola*, its *Falooda.*' Hamza corrects him.

'Okay, we will go and get some *Faboola*, happy, Muhammad?' says Ashoo in a cheerful voice.

'Yay!!' screams Muhammad.

Ashoo looks at me and asks if I would like to go with them, I nod in agreement.

'Give me 10 minutes, I will change and freshen up.' I reply.

As I comb my hair and put on some lip-gloss, Ashoo walks in the room and stands beside me and says, 'Hey beautiful, ready yet?'

I turn towards him and ask, *'What did you just say?'*

'Hey! Beautiful.' He repeats.

'Oh! *I want to be pretty, not beautiful.*' I reply with a smirk.

'What's the difference, Zo?'

I look at him from the corner of my eye and with an almost-devilish smile I say, *'You will never know.'*

Acknowledgments:

All praises to Allah. I would like to thank my darling husband, Nauman, for giving me a chance to find myself, by giving me my creative space, and for reading bits of this book. Thanks to my mom & papa for nurturing the rebel in me.

A big hug to my siblings: for putting me on a pedestal and bearing with me and my intellectual snobbery.

Heart-felt duas for my son, Ehraas, for reading the chapters of my manuscript and helping me with my punctuations, for designing the cover of this book, and encouraging me by saying "Mom, you are funny". My other two offspring, Eyhaan & Enshaal, for handling the logistical issues like charging my laptop and getting me things from the fridge.

The most difficult chapter for me to write was "Paradigm Shift", for which I thank my own Qur'an teacher for her many lectures,

Wael Abdelgawad for his inspirational writing that became the baseline for this chapter, and many wonderful friends who send continuous reminders about spirituality.

Last but not the least, a big thanks to Samreen, my partner in crime, for reading each and every word of this book with me and helping me in every possible way, this book could not have been possible without her help, can't thank her enough.

The most beautiful line in the book "I want to be pretty, not beautiful" was given by Anaaya, an 11-year-old princess, who inspires me every day.

www.ingramcontent.com/pod-product-compliance
Lightning Source LLC
Chambersburg PA
CBHW051427130726

47987CB00005B/1952